FRENCH VANILLA

By

David Broussard

FRENCH VANILLA

ISBN-13: 978-0578082912

I dedicate this book to my family, who has always been there for me, and never doubted my dreams, no matter how crazy they may seem. To all the beautiful women in the world I have met and have not met yet.

For it is your true beauty, that naturally inspires me.

Acknowledgments

I'd like to thank my loving Mom and Dad for all of there support, love and understanding. My kids, David Jr., Branden, Brittan and James for all there love and so much laughter throughout the years. My older brother and sister, Gregory and Christina for there love and guidance. I want to also thank all my good friends for there great friendship.

Table of Contents

Chapter One

It was a warm sunny morning in New Orleans, Louisiana where a young lady around 24 years old was getting up out of bed. Her mother walks into her room and greats her.

"Good Morning Frenchy", her mother says to her. She answers back "Good morning mama". Her mama tells her to hurry up and come eat her breakfast and walks out.

This tall, sexy, light skin and long hair young lady finishes her daily routine looking in her mirror and saying to herself, "Beautiful you are".

She starts for the breakfast table and looks at her phone. There is a text from her boyfriend Dirt that says "where u at".

Dirt is a nick name for Dirty South. A notorious thug from the projects, who she met back in the day that hooked her up doing drug runs when she needed some extra cash.

Frenchy sits at the table beside her mama and her mama ask her about when she is going to go back to school. She tells her that she is going to start soon and makes her a promise that she will.

They go on for a while about how dangerous it is in the hood and her mother says "when are you going to meet a nice young man and get married"?

She tells her that soon she will try to meet a nice guy and her mother goes on to say that you know that Dirty boy aint no good. Frenchy answers "I know mama, I know".

So they both finish up there oatmeal and Frenchy starts out of the house to meet up with Dirt.

She walks down the steps and gets in her bucket of a car and what do you know. The car won't start.

She calls Dirt and tells him "This damn car won't start again. I need to make some real money so I can go to school and get me a real car".

He tells her that he has some stuff happening and she just might get a chance to make some real cash soon.

She was used to making drops in town for fifty dollars here and there. It was just enough money to get her hair and nails done weekly. And get some new clothes every now and then. She would also bring some food home periodically to her mama that she so loved.

As she waited for Dirt to come around, a guy from the hood rides up on a bike looking at her strangely.

"What's up Frenchy"? He says to her. She answers back "Hey, what's up boy"?

He asks her if her car wouldn't start and if she wanted him to help push start it. She tells him no thanks and sees a joint in his ear and tells him to fire it up.

He tells her that she aint ready for this bomb shit.

"This is the fire" he says. She shouts back at him. "A bitch needs something right about now".

So he fires it up, takes a couple of hits and passes it to her. She takes a couple of hits and starts choking really bad like she was going to throw up or something. The guy one the bike starts laughing at her and tells her I told you this was the shit. She passes it back and he hits it again really long and hard.

As he passes it back in the car to her Dirt hits the corner and sees them smoking together.   Frenchy sees that Dirt is coming so she tells the guy on the bike to leave because Dirt is crazy and the guy says we just smoking, I aint doin nothin.

Dirt pulls up gets out of the car and walks over to Frenchy and says "whats happenin here"?

The guy on the bike says we just smokin a joint and Dirt pulls back and punches the guy so hard he knocks him off the bike.

Dirt tells him "Was I talkin to you fool" as he pulls out a gun form his pocket and points it at the guy on the ground.

Frenchy screams at him, "Dirt we wasn't doin nothing, don't shoot him". Dirt tells the guy to get the fuck out of hear and the guy gets up and hauls ass out of there on his bike.

"You always talking to some nigga" Dirt tells Frenchy. He puts the gun away and grabs her by the hair and tells her "You lucky I love yo ass or I would slap the shit out of you". Then he lets her hair go. She looks at him and says "I just got my hair done, you aint gone do shit".

Frenchy's mama calls out to the car "Dirt, you leave my baby alone". He tells her "I'm sorry, I almost lost it".

He looks at Frenchy and tells her to come on lets go get this money. They both walk over to his Benz and get inside. Dirt starts up the car and they pull off. Just as they turn left on the first corner he slaps her and tells her "Don't you ever tell me what I aint gone do bitch".

She sits there and holds her face in shock. She can't believe that this fool just slapped her. Then Dirt goes on to say "Baby you know I love you and I aint gone never let you go. Till death do us part hoe".

Frenchy sits there and can't really comprehend what just happened. Dirt had never acted like this. What was his problem?

They kept driving for about five minutes in silence and then he says to her. "Baby, I'm sorry. I got a lot on my mind today. I just invested twenty thousand dollars into some shit and I am really nervous about it. He pulls over to a warehouse and puts the car in park.

He looks her in the eyes and says baby you know I love you. I am really sorry. I will never hit you again" and leans over and gives her a kiss on the cheek. She looks at him with evil in her eyes and tells him "Mutha fucka, you better not ever put your hands on me again".

He tells her "I won't baby, I promise". He points out of the car and she looks around out of the window. She sees a girl poking her head out of the door of the warehouse.

"Who is that"? She asks. He tells her to go inside and get the stuff. I will tell you all about it in a few.

So Frenchy gets out of the car and goes inside this place. Inside she sees all kinds of new clothes on the rack. There are shoes and purses, all brand spankin new. Her eyes pop wide open and she gets very excited.

"Hi Frenchy", says the young lady. "My name is Diamond".

The girl tells her to go ahead and grab something for herself. She asks her one of each? Diamond says sure go head.

Frenchy grabs a purse and some shoes in her size. Then she notices the stuff on the table behind the girl.

The girl tells her so this is yours also. She points to a bag with some dope in it. Frenchy walks over to the dope and picks up the bag. The girl tells her "When you come back you can grab some more things for yourself girl".

She starts for the door with her hands full and the girl slaps her on her ass and squeezes it.

"You really got a nice ass girl" she tells her. Not expecting the slap on the ass, Frenchy tells her "Hey watch it but thank you".

She walks outside and puts everything in the back seat. Dirt asks her if she got the stuff and she tells him yhea, but you better check inside the bag.

He leans over into the back seat and looks inside the bag and says yhea baby, that's it.

Leans back up to the front seat and starts the car up. They pull off rather quickly and head for Dirt's place. As they drive down the street Frenchy has plenty of questions.

"So what are you going to do with it now" she asks him.

"I'm gong to sell it in the hood, it's from this guy in Los Angeles."

"That cost you twenty thousand dollars"? She asked him.

"Yes baby, it cost twenty big dollars". Then he tells her if he can pick it up in Los Angeles, he can get it for fifteen thousand and save five thousand dollars. Her eyes light up and he notices that she seems very interested all of the sudden.

He then asks her if she might be interested in making a pick up in L.A. She asks him how much would she be able to make doing it and he tells her you can make a thousand dollars every time you do it.

She immediately tells him yhea I'll do it. She has the look of money on her face thinking about all the things she could buy with one thousand dollars.

So they pull up to Dirts place and park. She grabs everything from the back seat and closes the door. He hits the remote to lock the car and they walk up to the door looking around as if they were both paranoid and then they go inside and close the door behind them.

Dirt ask her to lock the door as he sets his gun on the table.

He tells her to go ahead and roll up a joint as he points to a box sitting there on the coffee table.

So she goes over and sits down and starts to roll up a fat one. She pulls a big bud out of the box and starts breaking it down.

Crumbling the sticky green bud down, she notices that he is not a real neat type of person. He has clothes and dirty plates and cups sitting around that need cleaning.

She sees some old dirty socks in the corner that need washing.

So she tries to clown him by saying "You aint cleaned this place since the last time I was here with you. Wasn't that about two weeks ago"? and starts to laugh at him.

He looks at her from the kitchen and tells her "I been real busy lately".

She finishes rolling up the joint and ask him for some fire to light it up with. He tells her to look by the TV. She looks over at the TV and gets up to get the lighter.

Dirt comes out of the kitchen and ask her if she might be ready to go to LA soon. She looks at him and says "Hell yhea, a bitch gotta get her money".

So Dirt tells her that she might be going sooner than she thinks. She looks at him and says "I'm ready when you are".

He tells her as she fires up the joint that he has to get the money from this pack and he will be ready. She ask him about how long will it take and who is going to buy it and he tells her to stay out of grown man business.

"Just be ready when I say its time to roll to L.A." Dirt adds.

So they finish smoking the joint of some Cush and now there feeling really high. So Frenchy starts to think about sex. She reminisces about the last time they had sex. She reaches over across the table to grab the remote. She rubs her breast on his legs and rubs her hand up his leg.

Then she asks him if he has anything to drink in the kitchen. He tells her sure and gets up to go to the kitchen and she slaps him on the ass as he walks away.

She looks at Dirt as he walks back into the room with her drink and notices his bulge in his pants. She thinks to herself, I'm going to get me some dick.

As he gets back over to the couch she grabs his belt and pulls him over to her as if she was stopping him from sitting down.

He stands there with the soda in his hand waiting for her next move and she starts to unbuckle his belt.

After she is done with the belt she starts with his pants. Unfastening the snap on his jeans and then unzipping his zipper. Now he is getting excited waiting for her to do whatever it is she is doing.

She tells him I want to give you something to show my appreciation. She reaches into his pants and touches his stiff penis. Pulling it out of his pants, she strokes it and asks him "is it woke yet". He tells her "Yes baby, it's woke now".

She pulls his pants and his underwear down to his knees and grabs is ass cheeks. He steps up to her knowing what's next. And she licks the tip of his penis.

As she teases him by licking him, she slowly puts just the head of his penis in her mouth.

"Mmmmmmm", that feels good". He says.

Then she puts more and more into her mouth each time she strokes him with her mouth.   She then takes one hand and touches his balls and starts sucking and stroking him at the same time.

"Danm, that feels good baby". He says.

"You like that don't you"? She answers.

After sucking for a few more minutes she stops and gets up and tells him "Let's go to the bedroom"?

He leads her to the bedroom and they both start pulling off there clothes. Off goes there tops and they stare at each others naked chest. Then they both take off there shoes and pants.

Dirt stares at her beautiful body as she stands there in nothing but her black panties.

Looking at her long curvy legs and thick ass, he can't help but to think about eating her out.

He tells her "lie down and let me taste that French Vanilla cream baby".

She sits down on the bed and he climbs on top of her after pushing her down. He starts kissing her neck first. She loves it as she caresses the back of his neck.

She tells him "make me feel good daddy".

He then starts kissing her breast and tickles her nipples with the tip of his tongue. She moans and starts to grind against his hardened penis.

He eases down towards her moist vagina and kisses her around her neatly shaved pussy.

She begs him to kiss her. "Kiss it baby, kiss it".

He teases her by licking around her fleshy opening and tasting her juicy flavor that had oozed out of her soft wet pussy. He nibbles gently on her pussy lips one at a time. She can't stand it anymore and tells him to suck it.

"suck me, suck me baby" she cries. He puts one of his fingers inside of her slowly and she starts to moan louder.

"Mmmmmm, yes baby", she says to him.

After sliding his finger in and out of her a few times, he puts two fingers in and she tells him more, more. So he puts three fingers and she's humping and grinding pulling him toward her forcefully.

"Give it to me, I want it now", she tells him. He then starts to suck her sweet French Vanilla tasting vagina. He licks and sucks her clit as she squirms and moans.

"Mmmmmm, baby that feels so good", she tells him.

"Oh, right there" she whispers softly. He starts to lick her clit even harder as he can tell that it has gotten larger and firm. He shifts from slow and gentle to fast and wild as he sucks her wet hot vagina. She tells him that if he keeps it up, she is going to cum.

He slurps and smacks on her letting her know that he loves it as much as she does.

"Oh, baby. I'm going to cum. Yhea, I'm going to cum" she tells him.

"Oooohhhhhhhh, I'm Cumming, I'm Cumming" she cries out.

As she tightens up and grabs the back of his neck he licks and sucks her softer and softer. Then he stops and stands up. Pulls his underwear off and grabs his dick pointing it at her.

"Now you gonna get it Frenchy" he tells her.

"You gonna get it good". At that very moment there's a knock at the door.

"Aww Shit, Who the hell is that" he says to her. He grabs his draws and storms to the door very angry at who ever it is. He gets to the door and shouts "who is it"?

"It's me, Smokey" a voice answers.

"Aw, hell no" Dirt replies as he flings the door open.

Smokey tells him quickly "I saw your car out front, so I just came up, I didn't want to bother you but I just wanted a lil somethin. You got a five piece"?

Dirt was furious and started swinging at him without saying a word. He socks him in the eye, then the mouth. Then he swings again and socks him in the throat this time knocking Smokey down to the floor.

Dirt stands over him and looks down at him then he tells him.

"I told you mutha fucka, never knock on my got damn door unless you call me first nigga".

Smokey couldn't talk but waves his hands as if he didn't want him to hit him anymore.

Frenchy sees everything and shouts "don't Dirt, don't hit him anymore".

"Mind yo business bitch" dirt tells Frenchy and kicks Smokey in the head.

"This mutha fucka been disrespectin me to many damn times".

Frenchy screams at him "Your going to kill him" as picks up a large heavy object.

"No, Dirt. No". She cries out. Dirt stops and just looks at her with the devil in his eyes and at that moment she knew that she did not know this man who was her boyfriend for over six months.   Dirt looks at Smokey as he lies there on the floor choking and moaning and tells him "Don't you ever fuckin disrespect me in yo life again nigga" as he walks over to his pants and grabs something.

Frenchy thought he was getting Smokey some dope but what he pulled out wasn't no dope. Dirt had in fact pulled out a 9mm automatic pistol.

"You know I outa kill you fool, right now". Dirt tells him. Smokey starts to try and get up but puts both of his hands up and tells Dirt "Nooooo".

"Don't do it", Frenchy yells out to Dirt.

Dirt tells Smokey to get the fuck up and don't ever bring yo ass back unless you call me first.

"You got that mutha fucka" he adds! Smokey starts to get up and Dirt slaps him in the back of the head with the pistol "Pow". Smokey falls to the floor knocked out cold.

"Why did you do that" Frenchy asks Dirt.

"That mutha fucka always botherin me at the wrong time and I always give him a fuckin pass. Not this time, no way. Not this time" Dirt says.

Frenchy just stares at him in disbelief and shocked. Dirt then tells Frenchy to get dressed and go home.

So Frenchy gets up and puts her clothes on and runs out of the apartment. She gets to the corner and she hears some gun shots in the direction that she just came from.

She thinks to herself (No, I know he didn't kill him). She continues on her way home nervous and shaking. A stranger asks her if she is alright and she tells him yes, I'm alright. Thanks for asking though.

When she gets home her mother looks at her and can tell that something is wrong.

"Baby, are you all right". Her mother asks her.

"Yhea mama, I'm good." She replies. Then she goes into her room and lies down on the bed.   Later that night, Dirt calls her up on her cell and tells her to get ready for Los Angeles because you're leaving tomorrow. She answers back in excitement "really, tomorrow"!

"Yhea, your plane leaves at One P.M. so have your ass ready" Dirt tells her.

"Don't worry, I'll have everything ready". Frenchy answers back

"Don't worry; I'll be ready to go do the danm thing" she adds.

Later that evening she thinks about all the money she is going to be making and not about the dangers of getting caught.

She plans to buy new clothes, a new car; she even wants to buy her mother some new nice things. Then she thinks about paying for her education and using the money she makes to pay for that.

She thinks to herself, I want to be able to help people so I want to go to nurse school. As she looks in the mirror she tells herself, "I'm going to learn all about the medical field and maybe even get to marry a fine doctor".

After she finishes packing some stuff for her trip, she lies down and wonders what would happen if she got caught.

"Oh well, Dirt will help me out if something goes wrong" she assures her self.

"Hell, he better help me or I'll tell them everything is his and he made me do it".

She slowly falls asleep and dreams of finally making it and not having any more worries for her or her mother.

Chapter Two

When she wakes up in the morning, she is so very excited she lets her mother know that she is going to Los Angeles.

"Mama, Mama, I'm going to Los Angeles today and I'll be back sometime tomorrow" she shouts.

"Oh, is that right" her mother answers to her.

"Yhea mama, she then realizes that she can't tell her mother that she is going to pick up some drugs so she lies about the trip.

"I'm going out there for a interview for a new job" she tells her mother.

Her mother looks at her and tells her "Now you know that I wasn't just born yesterday, why you want to lie to yo mama baby".

Frenchy looks at her and says "I'm sorry mama, your right. I'm going to Los Angeles to make some money picking up some stuff for a friend".

Her mother looks at her knowing that she's going to do it for her boyfriend Dirt.

"You aint gone do nuthin fo dat boy Dirt are you baby? Dat boy is bad news for sho girl" she tells Frenchy.

"No mama, It aint like that at all. I promise I won't get into no trouble". Frenchy tells her mother.

She thinks about how she just lied to her mother and changes her mind about what she said and tells her mother the truth about the trip.

"Mama, I caint lie to you, I am going to L.A. for Dirt but just this time and I won't be doing it no more for that crazy boy".

Her mother answers her after she tells her the truth.

"Baby, I know you to good and I already know that you was goin to do something for dat boy. You just be careful and say a prayer before you go anywhere or do anything".

Frenchy goes into her room and finishes last minute packing. She grabs some cute clothes and some panties and bras.

"I'm gone need these" she tells herself.

Her cell phone rings and she sees it's Dirt calling her.

"Hello" she says.

"Hey, it's Dirt. You ready"? He asks her.

"Yhea, I'm ready". She answers back.

"O.K. Get over here". He tells her. She tells him that she will be right over and hangs up the phone. She looks into the mirror and thinks to herself, A scared bitch caint get paid.

She grabs her bag and starts for the door but stops in her tracks. Looks back at the mirror, drops her bag and walks up to it and starts to pray.

"Dear Lord, please protect me from all evil and watch over me as I leave on this trip. Also please watch over my mama while I'm gone and let me return home without harm. Amen".

She picks up her bag and walks out of the room into where her mother sits and says "Mama, I'm leaving now so you take care and I love you". She walks over to her mother and kisses her on the forehead. Her mother tells her goodbye and to be careful. Then her mama tells her I love you more baby and blows a kiss at her.

Frenchy walks out of the door and jumps into her car and tries to start her car but I wont start again. She turns the key and it won't even turn. The battery is dead as a door knob.

"Shit, this old piece of shit" she hollers out. She then pulls her cell phone out and calls up Dirt.

"Dirt, this old piece of shit won't start again; can you come pick me up"? She asks Dirt.

She hears him laughing on the other end of the phone and says to him.

"Aint nothing fuckin funny, what the hell you laughin at"?

He tells her "Nothin, I'm sorry. I didn't mean to laugh at you baby".

He tries to stop laughing and chokes a little bit. Then he tells her "I'll be over in a few. I'll pick you up on the way to the airport in an hour O.K"?

She tells him O.K. and hangs up the phone pissed off because he thought it was funny that her car wouldn't start.

She gets out of the car and storms back into the house and plops on the couch. Her mama walks in the room and says "What's wrong baby"?

"That dog on car won't start again. I am so tired of that piece of stank car" she tells her mama. Her mama looks at her and just shakes her head. "It must be a sign baby. You know sometimes the lord tells us things by showing us signs. Maybe the lord is telling you not to go" she says.

"I have to go moma, I promised I would. I'll be careful. You don't have to worry, I'll be careful" she tells her mother.

She leans over her mother and gives her a big kiss on the forehead. Then she goes into the other room and pulls out her cell phone and calls someone else up.

The phone rings and a deep voice answers.

"Hello" the voice says?

"Hi Good", she says full of excitement in her voice.

"I know we never really met and all but I'm coming out to L.A. and I thought we could officially meet and get to know each other.

Good answers, "Who is this"?

She tells him "it's Frenchy, the one from New Orleans you met online.

"Oh, how you doin Frenchy? I didn't catch your voice. I didn't know who you were or what to think" Good says.

"I'm doin good, just trying to let you know that I'm coming out there and was wondering if you wanted to meet up and officially introduce ourselves to each other" she says.

"Yhea, yhea, when are you coming out here" he asks her.

"I'll be our there today" she answers.

"I get in LAX at twelve noon. If you aint doin nothing you can pick me up at the airport. That way I don't have to catch no cab to my room" she tells him.

Goodnight starts thinking about her and her room and knows that if he gets into her room with her it's all over.

They met online on a singles dating site. They sent emails back and forth a couple of dozen times and then exchanged numbers.

Frenchy thought it would be safe because of all the miles between them. They even had phone sex one time in the middle of the night.

"So I will see you later at the airport right" Frenchy says.

"Yhea, sure babe. I will be there at twelve noon waiting for you beautiful" Good answers.

"See you later".

They both hang up and Good almost immediately calls up the homie Sticks.

At the same time Frenchy calls up her homie Lady.

Lady is a down home young mature lady. She has been there and done that when it comes to ladies in the hood. She has two kids and aint for no games. She can smell a player a mile away and will shoot him down in a second.

Good's phone answers with Sticks on the other end.

"Hello, Sticks". Good says

Sticks answers, "Hey, Daddy-O, Whats cookin"?

Good tells him, "I may need you to cover for me today, this fine ass Creole is comin out here from New Orleans and I'm gone spend some time with her today. So you know what to do".

Sticks answers, "I'm Hip. You down by law Good. I got yo back".

Lady answers her phone. "Hello".

"Hi Lady it's Frenchy, how are you"?

"Frenchy, I'm fine girl. How you doin"?

"I'm good, I just wanted to let you know that I'm gone be headin out to L.A. today" Frenchy tells her.

"What!" Lady screams.

"Yhea, I'm goin out there to try and come up girl. You know it's a lot of men and money out there" she says.

They both start laughing out loud. Frenchy tells her that she don't want to get into details right now but she will keep her in touch and tell her all about it.

Lady tells her "make sure that she is carful and watch your back. It's some scandalous, trifling dudes out there".

Frenchy tells her "they cant be any worse that these crazy ass project fools out here. Don't worry I'll be careful".

"Girl you know if I was goin with you we would have us a ball. Hollywood movie stars and Ballers all go our there to party and just lookin for some fun girl. You would have to pull me off of them girl". Lady tells her.

"Lady, you know I'm gone get me some and get one or two of those fine ass dudes sprung on this fine ass high yellow bitch. I'm gone get me some booty and everything that comes with it. But I'll tell you all about it ok, I gotta go. I'll send you a post card. Talk to you later Lady".

She hangs up the phone and goes to use the bathroom. In the bathroom she hears a car pull up and the horn blows.

"Damn", she says. I just sat down. Her cell phone rings and it's Dirt. She answers and tells him that she will be right out.

He tells her to hurry the fuck up, don't have my ass out here waiting all day. He hangs up in her face and she looks at the phone and shakes her head.

As she gets up and pulls her clothes up, she looks in the mirror and says to herself. "This fool really don't know".

She walks out of the bathroom and grabs her bag from out of the front room and tells her mother she is gone and not to worry.

"Love you mom". She shouts as she walks out of the door and heads for the car.

Dirt watches her walk towards the car and just as she gets to the door he unlocks the lock.

She opens the door and tells him to open the trunk so she can put her suitcase in the trunk.

Dirt gets out and opens the trunk and tells her "I hope you got everythang cause I aint comin back over here".

She puts her bag in the trunk and tells him "You always got something to say. You talk to damn much".

Dirt slams the trunk closed and tells her "Get yo ass in the car hoe, you the one always got something to say".

They both get into the car and they pull off away from her mothers house. As they drive to Dirts house he ask her if she is hungry and she says "Hell yhea I'm hungry, I aint ate nothin all day tryin to get ready for Los Angeles. L A, L A, here I come" in her excited voice.

Dirt looks at her and tells her "Don't get yo ass to excited, you goin out there to handle my business".

She looks at him with a smile on her face and tells him "Shit, I'm gone handle business, don't you worry bout that shit. I'm gone get mine".

As they pull into Bud's Broiler he ask her what you want? She tells him "I want a double with chili fries. He looks at her and says me two. You know we always did do things alike. He gets out of the car and goes inside.

While inside she pulls out her phone and text Good. The text reads "See you later, I cant wait".

Dirt comes out after a few minutes and they pull off to go to Dirts place. When they reach Dirts place he tells her to get the bag out of the trunk. She gets the bag out and shuts the trunk closed. They both go inside the building and go into Dirts place.

"You better make sure you do this right the first time cause if you do there is plenty of money to be made". Dirt tells her.

She nod's her head as if she agrees and they sit down and start eating.

"If this shit goes good we both gone be sittin on a fat ass bank roll around summer time". They keep on talking bout plans and things as they finish eating and she realizes that most of the talking that Dirt is doing is Braggin on how much he is going to be making and spending on him and she thinks that all she is getting out of it is some chump change compared to all the money he is going to be making.

Dirt gets up first and tells her come on lets go into the bedroom, I got a surprise for you.

Frenchy gets up and follows him into the bedroom. He grabs her and pushes her down onto the bed. She bounces on the bed and looks at him in the eyes.

She could never resist the sexual attraction that came along with the danger and excitement she knew that Dirt's life was all about.

He walks over toward her and starts to pull his shirt off. She tells him to take it off daddy.

He tosses his shirt over to the corner of the room and leans over her as if she was his prey.

She looks him in the eyes and looks down at his zipper and back into his eyes. He stands up and unbuttons his pants and pulls down his zipper. Drops his pants to the floor and steps out of them.

She looks at him and begins to smile. He then pulls his underwear off and tosses them at her. There he stands, ass naked. Penis hanging down his leg and Frenchy knows that she is about to get it real good.

Frenchy looks at him and tells him "come get this good lovin daddy" as she starts to take off her shirt.

He leans over her and starts to unbutton her pants. Pulls her pants off and then the panties come off next.

He climbs on top of her and starts to kiss her on the lips. Then he kisses her on the neck and then the shoulder.

As he starts to kiss her on the chest he starts to unfasten her bra. When he takes off her bra he tosses it over to the corner while he then starts to kiss her breast slowly.

He licks her nipple in a round and around motion. Her nipple starts to get hard and pointy.

She grabs his head with both hands by his ears as to guide him.

He moves from one breast to the other and she is starting to make moans as he then squeezes her breast firmly as he sucks them.

He starts to move slowly downward to her navel kissing and licking her along the way. She is enjoying every kiss and every moment as her yes moans start to turn into groans.

Down farther he kisses and licks her and just as she thinks he is about to kiss her pussy her goes around it and kisses her inner thighs one at a time.

Then he takes his fingers and pushes her vagina lips together and licks the outside of her lips.

Around and around he licks teasing her as he pokes his tongue inside of her lips short and fast. Then just as she thinks he is going to keep it up, he spreads her vagina lips apart and starts to kiss then lick then suck. Again and again. Licking, kissing, sucking her wet warm crouch.

He ask her if she likes it as if he didn't already know and she answers him "hell yhea daddy. I love it".

By this time he is hard and erect and he starts to climb up to kiss her breast again rubbing himself against her legs. Then he kisses her neck and up to her lips as she passionately and aggressively kisses his lips back.

"I want you". She tells him.

"I want you now. Fuck me, fuck me now daddy". She begs for it.

Dirt eases just the head in slowly and she groans for more.

"Yhea" she screams "give to me".

Dirt starts to ease himself inside of her slowly a little more and more every time. Then he grabs her forcefully and drives it inside of her all the way in deep.

she screams out "Yes".

As he has her legs up in the air toes pointed to the ceiling, he starts to pick up the pace a little and pumps her a little harder and harder with every stroke.

She loves it as she screams yes at the same time he pounds her deep all the way inside of her.

After about twenty to thirty yes's, Dirt pulls out and tells her to flip over as he stands up looking down at her.

She slowly starts to turn over and gets up on her knees. He slaps her on the ass and grabs one of her but cheeks with one of his hands as if he was opening up her asshole.

He eases his head inside of her wet warmth and starts to squeeze her ass cheek.

Just as he starts to push in and pull out, Frenchy starts to moan and groan some more.

Dirt starts to pump harder and harder as she lets him know that she loves it by giving him those yes sounds. All of the sudden he slaps her ass and she screams out loud followed by "Fuck me daddy".

He slaps her ass again and she screams out some more followed by fuck me daddy. He grabs her by her small waste with both hands and starts to really give it to her.

Pounding harder and harder, faster and faster, he is telling her "who's your daddy" as she answers "you are" again and again.

Frenchy starts to moan very loud and it sounds kinda like she is in pain. This turns on Dirt and he tells her "I'm gonna cum".

He tells her again "I'm gonna cum" and she starts to get louder and louder with the crying sounds.

She tells him "I can feel it daddy, cum on daddy, cum on".

Dirt shouts out loud "I'm Cumming" and pulls out and then shouts "OH!" and shoots his nut all over her ass.

Frenchy groans and moans as she wiggles saying yes, ooh yes, that's it, yes....

Dirt finishes ejaculating all on her ass and rubs his stiff penis up and down her ass crack.

Then he falls by her side on the bed and lays there as if he was trying to catch his breath.   Frenchy gets up and goes to the bathroom to get a towel to wipe herself off. She comes out of the bathroom with a warm towel and starts to wipe Dirt off and he tells her "That feels so good baby".

After she cleans him up, Dirt lays there and tells her to watch TV or something; he was going to take a nap.

In less than five minutes he was fast asleep but she was wide awake. She started to think about Los Angeles.

That's all she could think about was the big city and how it was going to be. She had never even left New Orleans her whole life.

As she was watching a program on TV, she started to fantasize about her having lots of money and socializing with celebrities at a party in Los Angeles.

Frenchy knew that if she was going to make something of herself this would be her chance. Los Angeles is the entertainment capitol of the world.

She looks at herself in the mirror and tells herself to don't think for one minute that it is going to come easy. A lot of young ladies have been there and done that, only to find themselves homeless and broke looking for stardom and only finding themselves selling there body for money.

She tells herself "I aint gone be no hoe.

I'm gone stay focused and make something of myself".

Then she goes into the bedroom and lies there next to Dirt. After a few minutes later she falls to sleep and starts to dream about being successful.

There she is in her dream driving a convertible sports car. She turns a corner and the police turn the corner right behind her. The police turn on there blue lights and she starts to speed up. The chase is on and she drives faster. She looses control of the car and the car crashes and explodes into flames.

She wakes up screaming and scared and realizes she is in Dirts place and it was only a dream.

She looks at the clock on the nightstand and thinks to herself, I have been sleep for two hours. She gets up and goes into the bathroom to use the toilet.

Dirt knocks on the door of the bathroom and ask her if she is alright. She answers yes.

He says to her, "I thought I heard you scream. It woke me up".

She tells him that she's alright and that it was just a nightmare. He tells her ok and that he was going to finish getting ready for the trip and then he was going to take her to the airport.

She tells him that she was going to try and read something and try to relax.

Dirt finishes packing the money into the suitcase and zips it up shut. Frenchy starts to read a book and ends up getting up and looking out the window not to long after.

Dirt gets out of the shower afterwards and puts on some clothes and tells her "this is it baby".

"We gone get us some real money like this". He looks at her and tells her come on baby lets go through the plan.

"First things first".

"You gone get through security and get on the plane".

"Then when you get to L.A. you gone call me and let me know you made it".

"Third, you gone get you a room and let me know what your room number is.

"Then I'm gone call my boy and tell him to take you the stuff and you give him the money when he gets there".

"Everything should be o.k. and go as planed".

"You don't have to worry about anything because this guy is like family and he got your back like I do".

"Me and him go way back and he owes me big time".

So Frenchy looks at him and says "o.k., Lets go through it".

"First, I get through security at the airport and get on the plane".

"Second, when I get to L.A. call you and tell you that I made it safe".

"Third, get me a room and tell you what the room number is".

"Forth, you gone call your boy and he is going to meet me for the exchange. Then I come back home the next day".

Dirt looks at her and tells her "That's it. Easy as pie. Lets go we don't want to miss the plane".

They get there things and double check the tickets and the bags. Then they start to head out to the car.

When they get out to the car, they put everything in the car and get inside.

Dirt starts up the car and they pull off. As they pull off, Frenchy takes a look at the neighborhood and tells herself when I come back I am going to be a new woman.

Chapter Three

They get to the airport and Dirt drops off Frenchy at curbside. He hurries her up and then he speeds off.

She checks her bags in with a skycap and then heads inside for the gate.

She gets through security with no problems and starts to head down the terminal to her gate.

She is so excited that she starts running her mouth to some young lady sitting in the same area about how this is her first time to Los Angeles.

Her and the girl kind of hit it off and before you know it they were just laughing and talking.

The airlines had then started asking all the passengers to start boarding the plane.

Frenchy gets up and waits in line to board and then she gets on to the plane. She moves down into the plane and sits right by the window as she looks out onto the runway.

The airline flight attendants start talking and asking everyone to please have a seat, they were about to take off.

Frenchy fastens her seatbelt and soon the plane starts to back out away from the gate area.

They enter the taxi way and the plane gets ready for take off.

Someone behind her says next stop, Los Angeles and the plane burst into full throttle and pushes Frenchy back into her seat.

Just as the plane starts to lift off, Frenchy starts to shout out "Ohh". Just like if she was on a roller coaster ride.

The plane climbs higher and higher till they reach about three thousand feet and levels out.

By now everyone is talking and the flight attendants are walking around passing out drinks and snacks to everyone.

"Would you like a drink young lady", a flight attendant ask Frenchy.

"Sure, I would". She replies.

The flight attendant is holding up a seven up and a coke. Frenchy looks at her and says do you have anything stronger than that.

The attendant ask her if she has any I.D. and she says yes I do thank you. The flight attendant looks at her I.D. and tells her "twenty four, thank you very much" as she hands back her I.D.

Frenchy says so what do you have? The flight attendant says "we have some white wine and some beer".

"I'll have some white wine please" Frenchy answers.

The flight attendant pours her some wine and she happily accepts it with a thank you very much.

After she finishes her wine she looks to the back of the plane for the restroom and gets up to go.

On her way she notices a nice looking young man and he notices her. He winks his eye at her and she smiles back as she walks pass him.

After she comes from the restroom, she is walking back to her seat and just when she passes the gentleman that winked at her, he reaches out and grabs her arm gently.

"Excuse me miss, but I was going to hate myself if I didn't at least ask you your name" he tells her.

She thinks to herself, "hmmm, that was kind of smooth" and tells him "Hi, my name is Frenchy".

His face lights up and he smiles at her and says, "That's a beautiful name, my name is Dulan".

"Very nice to meet you Frenchy, I love your suit" he adds as he looks down at her legs.

Frenchy is wearing a two piece suit.

A matching skirt and jacket with her very nice legs showing. She cuts him off and says "It was nice to meet you Dulan" and turns to walk away.

She tells herself "I don't want to seem to easy or starving and him being so fine aint helping the situation either".

She returns back to her seat and sits down only to notice that the guy across from her is staring at her also. So she gives him a smile as well and he nodes back at her.

He leans over towards her and says, "Excuse me, but are you in the biz"?

She looks at him and thinks to herself, is this an undercover police. Then she answers "Which biz is that?"

"The Entertainment biz. You know, are you an actress, singer, model or something like that." He asks her.

"No I am not, why do you ask?" she answers.

"Because you are so very beautiful and sexy I just thought that you might be in the business". He tells her.

She sits there and smiles at him and tells him "well thank you very much".

He knows from her smile that maybe here is his chance.

"My name is Jeffery but all my friends call me Jeff. You can call me Jeff because you're so pretty and I would love to be friends with you".

She reaches across the isle of the plane to shake his hand and tells him "my name is Frenchy, nice to meat you Jeff. So what is it that you do"?

"I'm a real estate agent, I sell homes". He tells her.

"Wow, you must make a ton of money doing that". She tells him back.

He looks at her and says with a grin on his face, "I guess I do pretty well for myself".

They both smile as if they knew at that time they were going to be friends and at least try to get to know each other.

"Maybe you can sell me my first home when I'm ready to buy". Frenchy tells him.

"I would be glad to do that for you since you're so pretty." He tells her with a grin of a wolf on his face.

At that time he then pulls out a business card out of his wallet and hands it over to Frenchy.

She reaches out to grab it and touches his hand as she takes the card from him and thanks him for the card.

Just the touch of her hand on his made him excited and he tells her that I noticed that no one is sitting there may I come over and sit with you.   She tells him sure you can. So he gets up and moves seats over to where she is sitting right next to her. Leans over to whisper into her ear and tells her.

"I am very attracted to you and when you touched my hand I could not help but to get aroused by your gentle touch".

She just looks at him and smiles. At that time, a flight attendant comes by and he asks her for a blanket.

The attendant brings them the blanket and he thanks her. He leans over to Frenchy and says into her ear give me your hand, I want to show you how much you excite me.

He grabs her hand and she lets him guide her hand over under the blanket to his hard stiff penis.

She is not surprised and she actually grabs it and squeezes it gently.

Jeff closes his eyes as she starts to stroke him slowly. He leans over to her and whispers into her ear, "Oh thank you so much, that feels so damn good".

He grabs her hand and tells her to stop. He then opens up the blanket as to cover both of them. Then he slides his hand over to her and slips it under her short dress up to her panties.

When he touches her crotch he immediately notices that she is warm and wet and she grabs his hand but doesn't pull it away, she just holds it right there.

He starts to wiggle his little fingers around her panties and she starts to spread her legs a little more than they were already.

Jeff manages to slide her panties to one side and slowly ease one of his fingers into her vagina.

Frenchy closes her eyes as he eases his finger back and forth in and out of her wet warm pussy.

She leans over to his ear and tells him "I don't believe this is happening".

He continues to finger fuck her right there on the airplane. He then leans over and gives her a kiss on the cheek slowly and then the neck and then she looks at him so he kisses her on the lips.

Just as he kisses her on the lips she tells him "I'm Cumming" and grabs his hand tightly and squeezes his wrist as she Cums all over his finger.

She opens her eyes and tells him to stop and pulls his hand away from her wet red hot pussy.

He looks at her and asks her "so will you join me in the rest room".

She looks at him like he is crazy but before she could say anything he gets up and starts walking to the back of the plane.

She hesitates at first but then gets up and starts walking after him as if she was trying to be inconspicuous.

By the time she gets to the rest room door she notices that it is cracked open and she didn't see him actually go inside so she opens the door slowly and there he is. Standing there waiting for her.

She eases into the rest room and he shuts the door and locks them both in it.

He reaches under her skirt and grabs her panties and pulls them down off of her. She helps him by pulling them half way down her legs.

He unbuckles his pants and pulls down his zipper. Pulls his pants down just below his ass and turns her around and then bends her over the sink.

He pulls out a condom from his pants pocket and slides it on quickly like a pro.

Then he tells her to open her legs and sticks just the head of his hard penis in slowly. The rest of his penis just easily slides right in as he starts to stroke slowly inside her warm wet vagina.

Frenchy cant believe that she is doing this and she loves it. He loves it too as he grabs her by the back of the neck and pumps her doggie style.

They exchange moans and groans softly as they don't want anyone to hear them but Frenchy is getting louder and louder and so is Jeff.

Jeff cant help but to slap her on the ass because it is so plump and round and she blurts out a loud OH! She tell him to fuck me daddy and repeats it a second time.

"Fuck me daddy".

Jeff then grabs her with both hands by the waste and starts to stroke harder and harder as she puts both her hands up on the mirror in the bathroom to stop from banging her head against it.

He then starts to ask her if she likes it as if he didn't know.

"You like it don't you" he asks her.

"Yes, Yes" she replies.

"Ooooh, that feels good baby" he tells her. She answers, "Yes, yes it does. Harder".

So after they exchange yes sounds for a few minutes, Jeff tells her "I'm going to cum baby".

She tells him to "Cum on. Cum on daddy".

Jeff starts to pump her with some long stokes and explodes a big fat nut inside her as he starts to slow down from the explosive climax.

Frenchy tells him "That's right baby give me all that good nut" as he gently stops and just holds it inside of her.

He can also feel her vagina contracting around his hard penis as if she was actually massaging his dick with her pussy muscles.

She lets her arms down from the mirror and pushes him back out of inside her. She turns around and grabs his rubber and gently pulls it off of his penis slowly.

He moans and tells her thank you so very much as he realizes that they are still on the airplane and pulls his pants back up and zips them shut.

Frenchy puts the rubber into the toilet and gets her self together and then Jeff ask her are you ready and she agrees yes.

Jeff opens the door to the restroom and leaves out first and then Frenchy leaves a few seconds after.

They both return to their seats and it seems that no one actually knew that they were even gone.

So they both sit there amazed at what had just happened. Frenchy tells him I don't believe that just happened.

Jeff replies "I have been flying for six years now and that has never even crossed my mind before. I don't believe that it just happened either. But it did and I am very glad and I will never forget it" then he pauses.

"And I will never forget you Frenchy" he adds as he looks her in the eyes.

She just smiles back at him and grabs his hand. Jeff reaches into his pocket and pulls out a second biz card and hands it to her.

"If you ever need anything, please feel free to call me up". Jeff tells her.

"I mean it. I am a single man and you are so very pretty. You really just don't know how much you just did for me. I mean I was built up for about two months". And they both start to laugh out loud.

Frenchy looks at Jeff and tells him "So I made a new friend and I'm glad. I was thinking on moving to Los Angeles to finish going to school and try to better myself".

Jeff assures her again that if you need anything just let me know. "I'll come runnin. You do want me to Cum right". And they both start laughing aloud again.

So they continue their conversation back and forth for a little while and soon they here on the speaker "We are approaching LAX and we will be landing soon".

The plane starts to descend slowly and Frenchy grabs Jeff hand. He looks at her and asks her if she is scared. "Are you scared"?

"I've never flown before" she answers.

"It's alright". He tells her.

"I fly all the time".

So the plane lands on the runway, taxis around, pulls up and parks at the gate. They both say there good byes and give each other a hug as they depart off of the plane.

Frenchy walks out of the plane and starts to head down the terminal.

She stops and looks to see how nice the place is because she has never been out of New Orleans. She then heads down some stairs to the baggage claim.

When she comes out of the turn style she sees Good holding a sign that says FRENCHY with one hand and some flowers in the other.

She walks up to him screaming his name "Good" and gives him a great big hug almost knocking him down as he drops the sign.

He gives her a kiss and asks her how are you doing? She answers "I'm great. It's so good to see you finally".

Good tells her you are so much prettier than you are on your pictures and she tells him thank you.

"Your chariot is waiting outside for you Darling" he tells her.

"I have to get my bag. It's on carrousel number one" she says.

They both walk over to carrousel number one and they hear a loud buzzer as the carrousel starts to turn around.

The bags start to cum out of the bag shoot and then she sees her bag.

"There's my bag right there". She tells Good and he grabs it from off of the carrousel and he tells her so the car is this way. She grabs his arm and they stroll together out of the terminal across the street to the car.

He puts her bag into the trunk and walks around to open her car door for her.

She looks at him surprised and tells him "Wow, no one has ever opened a car door for me before".

She gets into the car and he hands her the beautiful flowers and then closes the door.

Good walks around the car to the driver side, gets inside of the car and closes the door.

He leans over to give her a kiss and she grabs his face with both hands while kissing him in the mouth.

He looks at her and tells her "I like that". She tells him that there is more where that came from.

"So, where too?" Good ask her. She looks at him and says "I'm not sure. I don't have a reservation and I don't really know the area. Do you know of any good hotels here?"

"There's a few good ones right here by the airport" Good tells her.

"I'll take you to really nice one not to far away".

He starts the car and they drive off headed for the Hotel.

"Are you hungry?" Good ask her.

"Not really" she replies.

"Have you ever had chicken and waffles before?" Good ask her

She looks and him in a strange way and tells him "NO."

"Well, it's pretty good. You just might like it". Good tells her. "It's on the way to the Hotel so don't worry".

They pull into the parking lot of Roscoe's Chicken and Waffles and they both get out of the car and head inside of the place.

"I have to use the rest room first" Frenchy tells Good. "I'll be right back". Frenchy goes into the rest room and calls up Dirt.

"Hello Dirt, I made it. I'm in L.A. and I'm going to the hotel. I'll let you know what room when I get there".

"So everything is cool right?" Dirt asks her.

"Everything is cool. I'll call you back in a few minutes when I get to the room o.k.?"

Frenchy tells him and just hangs up the phone on him.

She walks out of the bathroom and Good is standing there waiting for her as she walks up to him.

"So, you want to try the chicken and waffles or you want something else". Good asks her.

"I'll try the chicken and waffles babe". She tells him. They walk up to the counter and a young lady asks them can she help them.

"Yhea, we want two chicken wings and waffles to go please". Good tells her.

"Would you like anything to drink or anything else?" the young lady asks Good.

"Yes, can I have a two percent milk" and turns to Frenchy, looks at her and ask her "what would you like?"

She tells him "I'll have an orange juice".

The young lady rings up their order and tells him that will be twenty one dollars and forty two cents.

Good reaches into his pocket and pulls out some twenty dollar bills and hands the girl two of them. She gives him his change and tells him that it will be about ten minutes.

So they both turn around and have a seat right across from the cashier and wait for their food.

While they wait, Frenchy's phone rings and she ignores it. It is on vibrate so no one can hear it.

Good starts to tell her about some of the pictures on the wall and how a lot of stars and celebrities always come there to eat.

Just then a famous rapper walks in and walks up to the cashier. Frenchy almost immediately recognizes him and starts to pat Good on the arm repeatedly. She leans over and whispers onto his ear "Is that" and before she could get it out the rapper looks at her table and says "Good, what's good with you man".

"Hey man, what's really goin on?" Good replies.

"Just getting some of dis crazy bird man" the rapper tells him. Hey who is this fine tender you got wit you?"

Good starts to say "Frenchy, meet one of L.A.'s finest". Frenchy immediately cuts him off and tells the rapper "I've seen all your videos, I'm a big fan" and holds out her hand to shake his.

"How do you do? Very nice to meet you", the rapper tells her while shaking her hand.

"Hey Good, I'm gone catch yall later man". Good answers "Alright Dog Pound".

Frenchy is in awe and she can't close her mouth. The cashier tells them that there food is ready and they get up to grab there bags and go.

They walk out to the car and Frenchy opens the door for herself and gets right into the car. Good walks around the car and he also gets into the car, puts the key into the ignition and starts up the car.

As there pulling out of the parking lot Frenchy is on Good like white on rice.

"I don't believe you know him" she tells Good.

Good looks at her and tells her "Maybe I can get you in one of his videos".

Frenchy grabs his arm and begs him "please, please, please get me in one of his videos".

"Don't trip, I got you babe". Good tells her.

So they pull up to the hotel and she tells Good, "This is nice, I hope that it aint to expensive" Frenchy tells Good.

"I'll make up the difference if it's too expensive for you" he tells her.

They pull up to the front door and pop the trunk to get her suitcase out of the trunk. Good grabs the bag and they both go into the lobby and walk up to the desk.

"Hello, how can I help you today" the front desk clerk ask them.

Frenchy tells the girl that she would like a single room. The girl asks her if it is for one or two persons. Frenchy tells her one. The clerk tells her that they have a single for seventy nine dollars a night and would that be smoking of non smoking?

Frenchy answers Smoking please because she wants to get her smoke on. She heard that the Kush out here in Los Angeles was the bomb.

The clerk asks her how many nights and Frenchy tells her only one night.

The clerk gives her a total and Frenchy gives her the money for the room. She gets handed a key and the clerk tells her what room she's in and gives her directions.

Good grabs her bag for her and they start off for the elevator which is right down the hall to the left of the lobby.

The elevator doors open and they enter the elevator and Good pushes the ninth floor button. The doors close and Frenchy looks at Good and asks him so what are we doing tonight?

Good looks at her and says well how about coming to my club and letting me show you a good time.

Frenchy answers "sure, that sounds great. I have to take care of some business first and I'll be ready in a few hours".

"I'll pick you up around nine tonight then".
Good tells her.

"O.K., I'll be waiting" Frenchy replies.

The elevator doors open on the ninth floor
and they both exit the elevator. Good looks at
the sign on the wall and tells her "this way".

They walk down the hall together and stop
at her room door.

"Here it is room nine eleven". Good says.

Frenchy puts the key into the slot and the
light changes to green. She opens the door and
they both enter the room. Frenchy looks at the
room and goes over to the window to open the
curtains.

"Wow, this is really a nice room" she tells
Good.

"I told you, they have really nice rooms
here". He answers back to her.

She looks at Good in the eyes and walks up
to him and grabs his hands. Holding his hands
she looks at him and says "I know your going to
make this a night to remember".

Good leans over and kisses her in the lips and tells her "You better believe it baby".

She pushes away from him and tells him not so fast handsome, I have to freshen up and take care of my business first.

"Business before pleasure. Right". Frenchy tells him.

Good looks at her and grins with excitement and tells her "I like your style Frenchy".

Good backs off and tells her that he will pick her up later. "You have my number just in case babe" he says. Frenchy tells him that she will be waiting and she can't wait.

Good walks over to the door and opens it. Just as he is walking out Frenchy tells him "Hey wait, aren't you forgetting something?

Don't you have something for me and what about dinner? A girl's gotta eat right".

Good tells her oh, that's right. He pulls out a bag of kush from his pocket and gives it to her.

"Your gonna love this shit, this is the show stopper. And I'll pick you up around seven o'clock then. Doe's that sound better?"

"Yhea, that sounds a whole lot better. I was so excited I almost forgot about the bud and eating" as she starts to laugh it off. "So seven o'clock it is then". Frenchy says.

"Alright, see you later" Good answers back and then walks out of the room.

Frenchy walks over to the window and just takes in the view of Los Angeles. She can't believe that she is really here.

Out in the distance, she can see the Hollywood sign on the side of the hills and to her it looks so beautiful. She reaches for her cell phone and calls Dirt to let him know she made it safe and what room number she's in.

Chapter Four

"Hello Dirt" she says before he cuts her off.

"Danm, it's about time hoe. What the hell took you so long? It's been almost an hour since you called me when you landed. Don't be playin no games bitch!" He tells her in an angry sounding voice.

"I aint playin no games. I had to get the damn room and I stopped to get me something to eat shit". She answers him back quickly.

"What's the damn room number shit?" Dirt says.

"I'm in room nine eleven at the Westin LAX" she tells him.

"So wait there and my boy gone come get the money and give you the shit right. He gone be wearing a blue LA Lakers hat. Don't open the door for anyone else and he should be by his self.   If he aint by his self don't open the door. You got that?" He tells her loudly.

"I got it, shit". She answers.

"So call me when he leaves and you got the stuff." He tells her and says bye and then the phone hangs up.

Frenchy knows that she has a little time so she goes into her bag and gets some clothes and underwear out.

She goes into the bathroom and starts the hot water for a nice hot bath. She puts some bubble bath that she brought from home into the tub and starts to take off her clothes. There she stands ass naked by the tub looking into the water.

"Something's missing" she says to herself.

She goes into her suitcase and gets out a candle and lights it up. Pulls out some papers and rolls a joint then she gets an ash tray.

She walks over into the bathroom and puts the candle on the end of the tub.

"Now, I'm ready" she tells herself. She gets into the tub with the bubbles everywhere and slides down all the way in up to her neck.

"Mmmmmm, this feels good" she says as she reaches for the ash tray. She grabs the lighter and lights up the joint. Takes a hit, blows it out slowly and starts to choke very seriously.

"Danm, this is the shit" she says to her self as she looks at the joint. I shouldn't be smokin this yet. I need to handle my business first.

So she puts the joint down in the ash tray and starts to feel a high coming all ready.

She just soaks there for a few minutes and lets the bubbles take her away. About fifteen minutes pass and she is really relaxed now from the kush and the hot bath.

All of the sudden there's a knock on the door. She jumps up and grabs a towel off of the rack and raps it around her wet body as she walks to the door.

She looks out of the peep hole and sees a guy in a blue LA Lakers hat.

"Just a minute" she tells him and wraps the towel around her tightly. She opens the door and tells him to come on in.

"I didn't expect you so soon" she tells him.

"Danm, you fine" he tells her as he enters the room and closes the door behind him.

"My name is Hound baby, what's your name?" he asks her.

"Hold on Hound, I have to put on some clothes first. You caught me at a bad time". Frenchy tells him as she walks into the bathroom.

"Shit, I'd say I caught you at the right time" Hound tells her as he has a seat in the chair.

Frenchy puts on some clothes and comes out still a little wet. She looks at Hound and says "So, you got something for me".

Hound looks at her and says "Yhea baby, I got something for you and you can have all you want too.

He puts a bag with something in it on the table and unzips it open to show her the dope inside.

She walks over to the bed and gets the money and then she puts it on the table next to the dope.

"So you gonna tell me your name you pretty thang you" Hound asks her.

"My name is Frenchy, Mr. Hound" she tells him.

Hound looks at her and gets the money bag off the table, zips it up and tells her "Look, I know your Dirt's girl and all, but let me show you a good time since you out here and all. Dirt aint got to know nothin. I promise I won't tell him. I just want to show a good time you know what I'm sayin. I just want to see that pretty smile of yours some more".

She looks at him and says "I don't know, I better not. Dirt wouldn't like it and he would kill me if he found out" Frenchy tells him.

"Shit, Dirt would kill us both if found out. Even if nothing happened at all" Hound tells her. And they both start laughing it up.

"Look at that smile, your beautiful Frenchy" he tells her.

"Dirt never tells me that. He is so abusive, it's a shame" she tells him in a sort of embarrassing way.

"If you were my lady I would never abuse you, verbally, physically or sexually". Hound tells her in a caring way as he looks her in the eyes sincerely.

Frenchy looks at Hound and asks him "Do you really mean that or is that some of your L.A. game".

"No, I really mean it and if you give me a chance to prove it to you I would show you" he answers her back. He then walks over to her and grabs her by the hand and tells her "Just trust me beautiful".

Hound feels like he has fallen in love at first site and Frenchy feels just what he is saying to her. She also is thinking maybe this is what she was waiting for.

Hound has money and she could be on her way to a better life. She looks into Hounds eyes and tells him "You better not be playin with my emotions" with a smile on her face and pulls her hand away from him.

"So finish getting dressed and I'll be right back to pick you up and I can show you around a little bit" Hound tells her.

"I'll be right back in about thirty minutes" he says as he picks up the money and walks over to the door.

As he gets to the door he turns around and looks back at her. There she stands looking at him with a grin on her face.

He smiles back at her as if he is satisfied and opens the door, walks out and shuts the door behind himself.

"Shit, what am I doing" she asks herself. She walks over to the window and looks out to the hills at the Hollywood sign.

"Dirt doesn't love me anyway and a girl gotta look out for herself". She tells herself as she turns away from the window.

She walks over to the joint, picks it up out of the ash tray and fires it up again. She takes a big hit and starts choking again.

"I'm gone get mines. Shit!" she thinks to herself.

She grabs her cell phone and calls up Dirt. He answers.

"Hey". He says

"Hey, I got it and everything is cool" she answers.

"O.K., so all you gotta do is get back to New Orleans tomorrow. You got that". He tells her.

"I got it" she answers back.

"Don't do anything stupid while yo ass is out there" he tells her.

"I wont, and don't worry about it" she tells him back.

"I'll see you tomorrow. I'm gone to get some post cards". She tells him and hangs up the phone in his face.

She thinks to herself "That fool must be crazy to think that I aint gone take advantage of my opportunities. She dances over to the chair and picks up the TV remote control. Turns on the TV and changes the channel to some local news.

On the news she sees how crazy L.A. is with all the drama about drive byes and murders, home invasions, Police excessive abuse and robberies. She realizes that it aint much different than where she comes from.

Thirty minutes pass in no time and there's a knock on the door. She walks over to the door looks through the peep hole and there's Hound. He is back in thirty minutes, just like he said.

She hesitates to open the door but does after a moment. Hound walks right in as she watches him walk passed her into the room.

"So, you ready sexy" he tells her.

"Yhea, just give me minute to do some finishing touches" she tells him.

"Baby, you aint got to change a thang" he says as he looks her up and down stopping at her ass.

She goes into the bathroom and brushes her hair and puts on some lip stick. She comes out of the bathroom and walks toward the door and tells Hound "I'm ready".

"So you gone take me to the mall?" she asks him.

"Yhea beautiful, I'm gone take you where ever you want to go with yo fine self" he tells her as she blushes.

They both walk out of the room and she pulls the door shut to make sure it's locked.

They both get down to the car and Frenchy tells Hound "Wow, you have a nice car".

"It better be nice, it cost me seventy thousand dollars" he replies.

He opens the door for her and she gets inside then he closes the door.

He walks around the car and he gets inside the car, puts his key into the ignition and turns the key. The engine starts and he asks Frenchy so if you don't mind, let's hit some corners first and let me show you around town.

They kinda burn rubber out the parking lot as Hound is trying to show off the power of the car.

First stop they make is by one of his homies house. His homie comes out and gives him a bag of lethal Kush and he passes it to Frenchy.

"Frenchy I want you to meet a good friend of mine, Wolf. Wolf this is my new friend and soon to be lady Frenchy" as he leans over and kisses her on the cheek.

Frenchy looks at him like whatever, and says "nice to meet you Wolf". Wolf answers back "The pleasure is all mines".

He looks at Hound and tells him that he better make her his lady cause if he don't I sure the hell will and starts laughing as he backs away from the car.

"So I'll catch yall later man, I got some thangs to do" he tells Hound and runs around the car and tells Frenchy "nice to meet you baby".

"Likewise" she answers back.

Hound takes off and he tells her to roll up some of that shit. Thats the Ooh Wee baby. I know you aint had none of that shit.

They later pull up at a liquor store and Hound jumps out and ask Frenchy what she wants to drink. She tells him to get her some water and he looks at her and says "Yhea, right".

He goes into the store and comes out with a bag. He gets into the car and hands her the bag. She opens the bag and pulls out some ice and some cups first. Then she pulls out some cranberry juice and then some Grey Goose.

"I know you don't expect me to drink this right now" she says to Hound with an attitude.

"We aint got to drink all of it. Just a taste to go with the Kush baby" he tells her. So she looks at him and says what the hell. They sit there in the car and roll up some of the Kush that they got from Wolf and make a couple of drinks. They pull off from the liquor store and he tells her "Next stop the Mall baby".

Frenchy lights up the joint and passes it to Hound. Then she chases it with a drink of the Grey Goose and Cranberry.

"Now this is livin" she tells Hound.

Hound hits the Kush and also chases it with a sip of the drank. "Baby, we gone be right when we get to the mall" he tells her as he banks a corner and smashes the gas pedal. She looks over to the dash board and ask him how fast is this car anyway?

He looks at her and says "Shit this mutha fucka can go a hundred and fifty no problem". She just looks at him and smiles. He looks at her and asks her "You want to drive it"?

"Are you serious"? She answers.

"Yhea, I'm serious". He pulls over and gets out of the car and opens her door and tells her to come on.

She gets out of the car and walks around to the driver side and gets in. she adjust her seat and buckles her seat belt. Puts the car into drive and slowly takes off.

"Man, this is so nice" she tells Hound as he just sits back and lights up the joint.

"When you get to the next light make a left and keep straight till you get to the mall" he tells her.

For some reason cars are stopping and trying to get her attention, even with Hound in the car. I guess that's L.A. for you. Dudes be houndin ladies with the paper.

Hound passes her the joint and she hits it again and chokes like crazy so he passes her the drank.

"Here, sip on this" he tells her and she takes the cup and sips it.

So they arrive at the mall and Hound tells her to park anywhere. She pulls into a parking spot and puts the car into park while turning off the engine. She hands Hound the keys and leans over and gives him a kiss on the cheek.

They both get out of the car and start to walk towards the mall entrance. Hound grabs her hand and they walk together holding hands looking kind of cute together. Hi knows after she kissed him that he really likes her and she is starting to really like him.

As they enter the mall they look at each other and say I'm fucked up and agree with each other right.

When they get into the mall Hound goes right into the first ladies store he sees and tells Frenchy that she can get what ever she wants. So she goes over to the new arrivals section and starts to browse. A store clerk comes over and ask can she help so Frenchy tells her yhea I want to try something on. "Where is your changing rooms" she ask the clerk.

She points to the back of the store and Frenchy takes some clothes over the change area. Hound stands there waiting until she comes back out and she looks amazing.

"How do I look" she ask Hound.

"You look gorgeous" he tells her as he reaches out to take her hand and turn her around.

"I'm sorry but your ass looks amazing in that outfit" he tells her with a giant smile on his face.

She hits him on the arm as if to let him know that she loves his compliment.

"You so crazy" she tells him.

"I'm buying that for you" he tells her.

She goes back into the dressing room and comes out in a new outfit. This time it is a one piece suit with a zipper in the front and made out of stretch material to show off every curve that a woman has.

"Oh My Goodness" he tells her.

"I'm in love" he says to her looking like she was a sexual goddess.

"You can leave that one on if you want to" he tells her and even the store clerk tells her that she looks good in that outfit.

Her cute face and small waste just adds flavor to her sexy, shapely full figured body.

Hound goes up to her and grabs her by the waste and pushes up against her to rub himself into her sexiness.

He almost immediately gets an erection and he wants her to know it.

The clerk walks away as if she knows what he's trying to do. So they get a little playful in the store and she starts telling him to keep that thing away from me giggling and then she grabs it, looks at him and tells him that it's hard.

Hound at that moment knew that he was going to get some of that ass. But for some reason he knew that he wanted her to be his girl for sure.

So they pay for the clothes and walk out of the store holding hands again.

As they start to walk through the mall a couple of women walk up to Hound and say hello and ask who is his friend.

Hound immediately tells them none of your damn business. One of the ladies use to be his girlfriend and is obviously extremely jealous.

All she could do is tell him how good he looks and how he doesn't know what he's missing.

Hound walks away with Frenchy holding hands and Frenchy tells him "You want me to get in her ass". Hound looks at her in surprise and says "No baby, she aint even worth it" as he shakes his head.

Frenchy tells him "I'll fuck that bitch up if you want me to".

"Naw babe, I can handle my own ex problems" he tells her as they head toward the jewelry store.

So they walk into the jewelry store and Hound goes up to the salesman behind the counter.

"Hi, how are you" Hound says.

"Fine, thank you" the clerk answers. "How can I help you" he adds.

Hound pulls out a ring from his pocket and ask the clerk how much could he get for the ring on an upgrade. The man reaches out and takes the ring to look at it. Hound tells him that he did buy it here and its three karats and 18 karat solid gold.

The clerk tells him to wait just a minute and reaches over into a drawer to pull out a loop. He puts the loop up to his eye and looks though it at the ring.

"Very nice" the clerk tells Hound.

"You want me to pull out my certificate" Hound asks him.

"No, that wont be necessary sir" he answers. "So you want to upgrade".

"Yhea, what am I looking at" he ask the clerk. The clerk answers back "Just look around and see what you like. I'm sure we can work something out" he tells Hound with a smile on his face because he knows that this ring was custom made and not something that was bought from the counter.

He takes Frenchy to the glass where the rings are and ask her if she likes anything. By this time she is all wrapped around his arm like a tight sweater.

"I know its kinda early for something like this but I have this ring that belonged to my ex and I don't want to give it to anyone else except for maybe you in the near future" as he smiles at her.

She has never seen anything so beautiful before so she ask him "How much did something like that cost"?

He looks at her and tells her that if you had to ask then you probably couldn't afford it.

"I will tell you that I had it custom made though".

She looks at something in the counter glass and says to him "I like this one".

The clerk comes over and opens the glass, pulls out the ring, looks at it and tells her that this ring is on sale for four thousand three hundred. "It is very nice".

She looks at Hound and says "That's too much money for that ring". Hound looks back at her and tells her no its not, that's a very good price.

Hound is trying his hardest to not tell her that the other ring that belonged to his ex cost fifty thousand dollars.

Even the store clerk is ready to burst and say how much the ring is worth. But the both stay cool and Hound gives him a wink.

They store salesman then changes the subject by saying "Ah, you two love birds make a great couple. Your future wife is so very beautiful" as he hands the other ring back to Hound.

He now knows what kind of style and taste Frenchy has so he can order a custom ring worth around fifty thousand dollars. The same price as the first ring he is going to trade in.

"Do you see anything else you might like" Hound asks her.

"Well this one looks nice too" she tells him as she points to a smaller size ring, knowing that it will be priced at a lower price than the first one.

So after looking at a few more items in the store Hound tells the salesman to have a nice day and he will see him later. The salesman waves at them both and tells them to have a nice day also.

They walk out of the store and Frenchy asks Hound if she can ask him a personal question. He answers sure you can.

"Do you believe in Love at first sight"?

He looks at her and says "Sure, I'm curtain that it happens all the time".

He grabs her hand again and they walk up to an escalator and go upstairs to a sports shoe store. They look around the store and he tells her to pick out some shoes for herself. She looks at some Nike's and ask a sales person to get her a pair from the back.

He brings out a pair of nines and hands them over to her to try on. She sits down and tries them on the they fit perfectly.

She stands up and takes a couple of steps turns around and walks back.

"I'll take these, if you don't mind" she tells Hound. He smiles at her and says "Do you see anything else that you like"?

She smiles back at him and tells him "No, babe. That's all".

They both walk up to the register with the shoes and Hound pulls out a folded stack of dub's and pays for them.

As he puts the rest of his money back into his pocket he reaches over and touches her on the ass and ask her if she has the munchies yet and she doesn't even say anything about him touching her ass.

"I got the munchies babe" he says.

"Me too" she replies.

"You want to go get some ice cream" he ask her.

"Sure, that sounds great" she adds sounding excited. They walk out of the store and she asks him what time is it. He looks at his watch and tells her it's about five o'clock she tells him that she has to get back to the hotel. She remembers that Good is coming to pick her up about seven.

"So do you have enough time to have some ice cream" he asks her.

"Sure I do" she answers back. But we have to get it to go so I can get back to the room.

On the way to get the ice cream Hound asks her "so after today will you take me serious and think about being my lady"?

She just smiles at first and tells him that they need to take things one day at a time.

"I just met you today" she says with a joking smile on her face.

"I mean, I aint tryin to play you for all the nice things you bought for me today but I don't want to feel like I've been bought" she tells him.

He looks at her and tells her "I just want you to know that I am serious about you and I wanted to show you. That's why I bought you some things today".

They reach the ice cream spot and before they get out of the car she leans over and says "Let me show you that I am also serious about you" and gives him a great big kiss on the lips.

He immediately gets excited and has an erection. Frenchy kisses him again just to put some icing on the top of it all. Then she grabs his crouch and starts to massage him.

He loves it and starts to caress her on her back and back of her neck as if he wants her to give him some head.

Chapter Five

He tries to push her head down to his penis but she won't let him.

"Lets forget the ice cream and go back to the hotel" she tells him.

As he starts up the car instantly and puts it into drive and says "Now that's what I'm talkin about".

They leave the parking lot rather quickly and go right to the hotel bumpin the sound system very loud playing a song that talks about how he can do it like this and do it like that.

Frenchy seems to know the song because she's singing the lyrics along with the beat and artist.

Before long they pull up at the hotel, park and get out of the car. Hound slaps her on the ass and she grabs his hand to hold it as they walk into the hotel together.

Frenchy grabs his belt buckle with one hand and pushes the up button on the elevator with the other.

The doors open and there they are, going into the elevator of the hotel and Hound caint wait to get up to the room.

He pushes Frenchy up against the wall as the doors close and pushes the floor of her room. He presses his body up against hers and starts to kiss her and then he touches her breast with one of his hands.

Then he grabs her ass with the other hand and squeezes it hard, kissing her mouth and licking her lips at the same time as she starts to moan letting him know that she loves it already.

Then she grabs his ass with one hand and rubs his penis with her other hand.

She tells him "I want you baby. I want you so bad".

The elevator doors open and they both fly out of it in very much of a hurry to get to the room.

The get down to the room and she reaches for the key inside her purse. She pulls the key out and opens the door and they both start pulling off their clothes right away.

First their shirts come off, then their shoes, then their pants and then they both grab each other in a mad passion frenzy of lust. They both want each other passionately so very bad.

Kissing each other in the heat of passion quickly becomes both of them standing there naked looking at each other. It is like slow motion as they both start to gravitate down on the bed.

She grabs his penis and tells him "Looks like someone needs some attention" as she starts to stroke his woody. She then bends down and starts to lick it slowly. Then she tickles the head with her tongue and before you know it she puts the head into her mouth, licking it and sucking it.

He grabs her hair and moves it to one side so he can see her at work.

"Baby, that feels so good" he tells her.

She starts sucking all the way up and down his shaft, stroking it with her hands at the same time.

"Damn baby, ooh, yhea, just like that" he tells her.

"I knew you would like it" she tells him quickly as she goes back to work on him.

He reaches down between her legs and touches her warm wet slippery slit. Then he starts to massage his fingers around her vagina lips and before you know it he slips a finger inside of her.

"Mmmmm" she moans back at him.

They continue to work on each other for a few minutes and then they both jump up and she goes right to her back as he climbs instantly right on top of her.

"Tell me you have a rubber" she says to him. And like a magic trick he has one in his hand ready for action.

She grabs his hard as a rock penis and he puts on the condom. Then she slides the head into her wanting wet hole.

"Ohhhh, yhea baby" she says as he slides it mostly in her. He adjust himself over her as he humps her a few more times and then once he gets adjusted, he goes to work.

"Oh, Oh, Oh" she says as he starts to pump her in an aggressive way. Then after awhile the pumps turn into pounding against her tight little wet hole.

"Ooh, Ooh, Ooh" she starts to get louder and louder as he puts his arms around her legs locking her in a position so she can't move away from him.

Harder and harder he pounds her wet warm pussy. She loves it and he knows it by the way she's grabbing his ears and then locking her fingers around the back of his neck.

He looks her in the eyes and asks her "Who's pussy is this"? She opens her eyes and focuses in on his eyes and tells him "Yours baby, it's yours".

He really starts to give it to her good and then she starts to cum all over his hard long penis.

She starts to say slowly "I'm gonna cum" and then a little louder and a little faster "I'm gonna cum".

Then she starts to scream "I'm Cuming, I'm Cuming" and locks her leg mussels as to squeeze Hound.

So he really starts to pound her pussy and he also starts to Cum with her at the same time.

They both scream in ecstasy together like they were recording a song "Ooh, Aah, ooh ooh, aah".

Hound down shifts to a slow grind and after a few mercy humps he stops and he can feel her vagina muscles contracting around his still hardened penis. Then he pulls out slowly and leans down to kiss her right in her mouth.

After they kiss slow and passionately, Hound lies on his side and touches her hair ever so gently.

She lies there next to him feeling almost high as the clouds and thinking to herself, "I really like this man".

Frenchy looks over to the clock and sees that it is almost time for Good to come and pick her up. So she tells Hound that she has to start to get ready. She had made previous plans and asked him to please understand.

Hound looks at her as if it was not a problem and tells her not to worry, he understands.

"Call me whenever you can babe". He jumps up and goes into the restroom and turns on the hot water in the sink.

Frenchy is watching him and can't seem to understand why there is no drama coming from Hound.

She sits up on the bed and waits for him to finish in the rest room. Just as she hears the water turn off she gets up and walks over to the restroom door. Hound is coming out of the bathroom and she's going in at the same time.

"I may be a minute in the restroom Hound, if you don't mind could you let yourself out" she asks him.

"Sure thing babe" he tells her and leaves a biz card on the table.

So she's in the restroom and Hound is about to walk over to the door when the doorbell rings, ding dong.

Frenchy comes out of the bathroom and looks at Hound. He shrugs his shoulders at her and then asks her "Does anyone know what room you're in?"

She looks at him and says "Yes, that's probably my friend".

Hound at that time tells her to tell him just a minute. She walks over to the door and asks "Who is it"?

"It's me" Good says back to her from the other side of the door. Then she tells him just a minute.

Hound ask her if they know what she is doing out here? She looks at him confused and he elaborates for her.

"Do they know you have all the dope here" he asks her.

"No" she replies.

"O.K, Let them in" he tells her.

She goes back over to the door and opens the door and Good walks in and he and Hound greet each other.

"What's up man" they both say at the same time almost sounding loud and friendly.

They seem to know each other and shake hands and give each other dap.

Good knows Hound and knows what he is all about. His money.

He knows that Hound is one of the most well known hustlers in the city, if not the top one.

"Goodnight, what you been up to man" Hound ask him.

"Aw man, I just been tryin to get my club elevated". Good answers back.

Hound looks at him and shakes his hand again and tells him "Let me know if you need anything man".

"Alright man, I'll do that". Good tells him.

"So It's going to be popin tonight right" Hound asks Good and Good shakes his head up and down quickly without answering back.

Hound starts to walk toward the door and tells Frenchy "Alright, so I'll see you later".

Frenchy tells him alright and he turns the door and walks out and closes the door behind him.

"So that's what your doing out here" Good tells her as he shakes his head side to side.

"So now you know" she tells Good. "Is it going to change anything between us" she adds.

Good pauses for a moment and then answers her "Naw, I don't think so. As a matter of fact, it kinda turns me on shit" as he smiles at her.

They both look at each other and start laughing.

"But on a serious note, I do want you to be careful" Good tells her.

"Don't worry, everything is under control" she tells him.

He looks at her and says "That's what I was afraid of".

Frenchy tells him to have a seat; she needs to finish getting ready as she moves into the bathroom.

Good turns on the TV and sits down on the couch, grabs the remote and starts flipping through some of the channels. He stops at an action movie and laughs a little at some of the shooting scenes.

So after about twenty to thirty minutes, Frenchy comes out of the restroom looking out a site wearing the cat suit that Hound just bought her at the mall.

"Damn, you look good baby" Good tells her as he stands up sounding very excited. He then asks her if she hungry and if so what does she have a taste for.

She looks at him in a very sexy way and walks over to him slowly switching her hips side to side and says "I have a taste for some beef".

Good looks at her and tries to keep his composure together.

"I got some beef for you baby" Good tells her and laughs.

"You better have some beef for me" she tells him as she backs him up against the wall. Then she grabs his crotch and tells him "Now that's what I'm talking about". She can feel that he is semi excited and is starting to get a boner.

Good tells her not to start something she can't finish and she takes her hand away from his crotch.

"So what do you really have a taste for baby" Good asks her again.

"I'm always down for some sea food" she answers.

"Come on; let's go get some sea food. I know a great place not to far from the club" he tells her.

So they start for the door and walk out and down to the car together. Good opens her car door for her and she tells him "I could get use to this".

They take off from the hotel and arrive at the restaurant. Good pulls up to the valet and they jump out and go inside the restaurant.

As they are being seated inside Good sees and old acquaintance sitting not to far from them. She also notices Good and his date Frenchy.

So they sit for a moment and Frenchy tells Good to get her something to drink, she has to go to the ladies room and stands up.

The old acquaintance sees her get up and knows that she must be going to the restroom. So she excuses herself from her table and follows Frenchy into the ladies room.

When girlfriend enters the ladies room, Frenchy is in the mirror doing what ladies do, making sure they look good.

"Excuse me, but the guy your with tonight honey is nothing but a dog. I just thought you should know" she tells Frenchy.

Frenchy looks at her up and down and says "Well that's good to know because I got my Cat suite on girl, meow" and they both start laughing.

"Don't worry girl, I aint even giving him none of this" and points her finger to the sky.

"I like you girl, what's your name" she ask Frenchy.

"They call me Frenchy honey" she tells the girl.

"My name is Darla. Nice to meet you Frenchy" she says.

At the table Good is sort of nervous because he saw his ex go into the restroom behind Frenchy.

They come out of the ladies room and Good sees that nothing is wrong and everything seems to be alright.

Frenchy comes back to the table and sits down, takes a sip of water and puts the glass back down on the table.

"That's some good water" she says as she smiles and puts the glass on the table.

Good looks at her and says "Are you alright"?

"Yes, I'm fine" she answers. "Just a little hungry maybe".

Good looks for the waiter and gives him the signal. He comes over and says "Hello there, are you ready to order".

"Yes thank you" Good answers. "We will have some Lump Blue Crab Cakes and two Walnut Mixed Greens to start Please".

He looks over to Frenchy and says "Is that alright"? She looks back at him and nods to say "Sure, that's fine honey".

Good looks back at the waiter and ads "Then we will have two Grilled Swordfish and Scampi Grilled Jumbo Shrimp combinations please".

The waiter writes down the order and winks at Good, "Would you like something to drink as well sir" he asks. Good looks at him and ask "What is the wine of the month"?

"This month we have the Mac Murray Ranch. It has a rich aroma and flavors of raspberry, cherry and boysenberry" he answers.

"We will have the wine of the month please thank you" Good tells him.

"Excellent choice sir" the waiter tells him as he adds the wine to there order. He takes there menu's and walks off to the kitchen.

Frenchy is very impressed by how well Good placed their order. Now she is really hungry.

So they sit there and Good tells her that he never thought that he would get to meet her and that he felt kinda safe with her being two thousand miles away. She looks at him and says "I was feeling the same way. I never thought that I would really meet you. That's the only reason that I sent you a nude picture of me. I didn't think that we would meet, we would be just online buddies".

"When I masturbated with you on the phone, it was just a thrill and I never thought that we would actually meet. But now that we've had cyber sex, I feel kinda comfortable around you and even kinda turned on by the whole thing. Just thinking about it makes my panties wet". She tells him.

"So I have to tell you also that you really turn me on in person as well as over the phone" Good tells her.

"So now that you're here in Los Angeles, what do you think" he ask her.

"It is so nice out here" she tells him. "The weather out here is unreal. All the nice cars and people all dressed up and its just like in the movies" she says.

Good looks at her and says "It's not all what it seems to be. A lot of people just live day to day on nothing but trying to look the part and talk the part but many cant afford the things that they have. It's like a barrel of crabs and every one of them is tying to get to the top and they don't care how they do it. They just pull who ever or what ever down and out of the way".

By this time the waiter brings them there appetizers and some water.

"There you are sir" the waiter tells them.

"Thank you sir" Good answers.

Good tells Frenchy to dig in, this is going to be good. So she starts on the salad and tells Good "This salad taste great".

"Wait until you taste the Blue Crab Cakes" Good tells her with a smile on his face.

They both seem to be very content with each other but Good is a Player and he knows that this is just another one of his victims.

She is fine and also has a hell of a body. But we create our own realities in our own minds. Tonight, Good is just going to take what she has to offer. Her sexy ass body.

So they finish the appetizers' and the waiter brings out the main feast and sits there plates on the table.

"Wow, look at that" Frenchy says.

"It tastes better than it looks" Good tells her.

Frenchy looks at Good and says "Do you taste better than you look also"?

Good almost chokes on his wine and tells her we will just have to see wont we.

So they finish there lovely dinner and wine and sit there for a moment talking. Then Good tells her "So it's a little early but I always get to the club early. Are you ready"?

"Sure" she answers.

Good signals their waiter and he brings the bill. Good pulls out a credit car to pay for it and Frenchy is curious how much it is, so she grabs the bill.

"One Hundred Forty Five Dollars" she says as she looks Good in the face.

"You see what I mean by what I said earlier. I can't afford that" he tells her. "But for you baby anything" he says with a smile on his face.

"When you ask me years later, where was our first date, I will definitely know were it was" he tells her with a big grin on his face.

All she could do was smile back at him with her beautiful bright eyes.

The waiter comes over and grabs the bill and Good tells him that his tip is added on to the total. The waiter goes and pays for the bill and brings Good his Credit card back.

"Thank you sir and have a great evening" Good tells him as they get up and start for the door. They get into the car and off they go to the club.

Chapter Six

They arrive at the club and go inside to find that no one else is there yet. Good shows Frenchy around the club and they find themselves at the DJ Booth. Frenchy starts to play with the mixer and the control knobs.

"I always wanted to be a DJ" she tells him.

He walks up behind her and takes her arm and puts her hand on one of the turntables as if he is trying to show her how it's done. She acts like she's mixing and Good makes the sound of a DJ scratchin.

They both start laughing really hard and next thing you know Good is all up against her soft ass letting her feel his penis sticking out from his pants and it's getting so hard.

Frenchy reaches back behind her to grab what she feels on her ass and finds Goods hard erect penis.

She turns around and goes down on him right there in the DJ booth. Then she unzips his pants and pulls out what he finds soon in her mouth. Good thinks to himself "She don't waste no time at all".

Frenchy goes to serious work on him as Goodnight backs up against the wall.

"That feels so good baby" he tells her as he grabs her hair from the back of her head.

Frenchy never says a word as Good tells her Yhea, and Wow. He also lets her know by grinding her mouth every now and then that she is doing very well with him inside of her mouth.

She works his shaft as she sucks his head too and he loves it. She can feel his hard wood getting harder and harder as she sucks and strokes him at the same time.

Just as she feels his throbbing penis getting ready to cum, she tells him "I want you to cum in my mouth".

Just by hearing her say that, it made Good reach his climax and he tells her I'm going to cum.

"Catch it baby" he tells her as she strokes him softly.

"Catch it baby" he says again and this time he Cums inside her mouth and she never misses a beat. Sucking and stroking him, she drains his entire nut out from his penis. He finally pulls himself out and away from her.

"You are really something else" he tells her.

She gets up and starts walking toward the restroom. She enters the rest room and spits out what ever is left form his nut that she didn't swallow. Then she rinses out her mouth.

She comes out of the restroom and walks over to Good and tells him that she hopes that he liked it. As if she really didn't know.

"You got damn Skippy I liked it" he tells her with a grin on his face. She kisses him on the cheek and has a seat at one of the table's right there.

"I have some work to do baby. Make yourself a drink if you want to, I'll be right back" Good tells her.

She just sits there and thinks about her whole day and what has transpired.

She thinks about Hound and how much money he seems to have and then she thinks about Goodnight and what he said about everyone trying to act like they got it all and really don't have shit.

She likes Good, but she really likes Hound. She just sits there and thinks about them both for a minute.

Good comes out after about fifteen minutes and meets her at the table.

"So did you want a drink or something" he asks her.

"No, thank you baby" she replies.

"So my boys will be here soon and we gone get this party started right" he tells her. She gives him a big smile and tells him that this will be her first time at a L.A. party and she is going to have a blast.

So Good makes her and himself a drink and the rest of the club workers start to arrive one by one and get the wheels rollin.

The doorman comes in and walks right over to Frenchy and introduces himself.

"Hello there beautiful, my name is Big" he tells her with a big smile on his face. She looks at him and there he stands six feet and eleven inches tall. Two hundred and sixty pounds, all mussel and looks like he don't play that at all. Not someone you want to get on your bad side.

Frenchy introduces herself to Big.

"Hi, my name is Frenchy. Nice to meet you Big" she tells him.

"Your new around here, aren't you" he asks her.

"Yhea, I'm not from around here. I'm here with Good". She answers to him.

"Oh, o.k. So let me know if you need anything. Any friend of Good is a friend of mine" Big tells her as he walks away slowly going toward the door.

It's almost eight o'clock and the club will open up at that time. So the ticket person is in her booth and the DJ is in his booth and the bartenders are behind the bar and the waiters and waitresses are ready to serve.

"My band will perform around ten o'clock" he tells Frenchy and she looks surprised with a smile on her face.

"Well this is a real treat" she tells Good.

"I didn't think I was going to see you do your thing".

So the lights are dim and there are candles lit around the club everywhere. One section of the club has a red light effect going on and the other side is a kind of purple haze darkness. The DJ starts off playing some soft, hard foot song where the guitar and sax sort of dual each other.

The doors open and the party begins right at eight o'clock on the dot. The first couple of people in the club go right to the bar and take advantage of the in before ten bargains. That would be all drinks two dollars before ten, chicken wings and potato skins also two dollars each.

So the place gets packed fast and the crowd is jumpin with drinks, food and some good music by DJ Sexy. Good is all over the place saying hello to all the regulars that come to the club every week.

Frenchy seems to not be doing so bad herself with guys all on her sexy ass like white on rice.

One guy keeps on her like he wont take no for an answer. Good walks up and tells the guy that the woman is with me. He recognizes Good and tells him "I am so sorry man, didn't know that the lady was with you man".

Good tells Frenchy that if she wants to dance she can and she looks at him with an "are you crazy" look.

She whispers into his ear "these some thirsty ass fools up in here" and Good just laughs and smiles back at her. He tells her that he will be right back and waves down a waitress to come over.

"Give her what ever she wants" he tells the waitress. She looks over at Frenchy and asks her what would you like?

"I'll have an Escalade please" Frenchy tells her. She looks at Frenchy and says "what is an Escalade".

"It's a Cadillac with a shot of Padron" she tells the waitress. The waitress looks at her and rolls her eyes and as she walks away she says "Got it Honey".

So Frenchy gets her drink on and the night is going just fine. It's almost ten o'clock and Good comes over to Frenchy and tells her that she can come sit close to the stage of she wants to. He grabs her hand and guides her across the floor to the front of the stage. He pulls her chair out and lets her sit down at front stage.

"You gonna like this" he tells her and turns and walks away heading for back stage. He gives the DJ a sign and the DJ introduces the band.

"Good evening Ladies and Gentlemen. Tonight we have a special treat for you all. For your enjoyment we have some live entertainment by the smooth sounds of yours truly. Mr. Goodnight.

The drummer counts off the song "one, two, three, four" and the band starts jamming some upbeat funk.

Good is on the sax, and they also have keyboards, drums, bass, guitar and trumpet and a female vocalist. The crowd seems to like it as they start to dance and party on the dance floor, shaking there groove thang.

Frenchy loves it so much that she even gets up and starts dancing. Some guy standing close to her moves over towards her and starts to dance with her. Good watches her get her groove on and thinks to himself "that drink done kicked in now".

It's going down in the club and everyone is having a great time except for one young lady standing close to Frenchy.

Frenchy cant help but to hear her get louder and louder, talking about some bitch over somewhere stole her man. She gets so loud that just before she moves away from Frenchy, she hears her say "I'm gonna wup that bitch ass". And that's when she starts waking to the other side of the stage and gets in some other girls face yelling.

"Bitch, It aint over yet. He still comes to see me" the girl tells the other.

"Who you callin a bitch" she replies and the sparks start flying. They start swinging at each other and pullin each others hair.

One girl starts to get some good licks in while she holds her hair in one hand and clocks her in the face with the other hand. That's when she rip's her shirt off and then the other girl rip's the other girls shirt off too.

There they are, two grown ass women fighting in the club with no shirts on. Both of em aren't even wearing a bra. We got tittes bouncing all over the place while they swing back and forth at each other.

That's when Big comes out of nowhere and grabs em both at the same time. One girl in one arm, and the other one in the other arm. Lifts them both up and carries them both out of the club with a quickness as they both kick there legs saying "put me down, put me down".

Out the front door all three of em went and Big tosses the two girls out into the street and screams to them "No Fighting" and turns to go back to the door and stands there with his arms folded together looking tough.

Meanwhile inside the club, Frenchy is standing there with a shocked look on her face.

Good walks up and asks her if she is alright.

"Yhea, I'm alright. That shit was crazy. Hoes be really on one out here" and starts laughing.

Good tells her don't trip, it might get better. There was some gun shots in front of the club about a week ago and everyone was running out the back way.

"One time this guy shot this dude right in the head and killed him" he tells Frenchy.

"What" she replies?

"Not for real. I'm only playing" he tells her and she hits him on the arm and relaxes a little bit.

So the club continues on with everyone there having a good time and before you know it, one of the girls is back inside the club. Frenchy hears her tell her friend that the other girl left so Big let her back inside.

Frenchy is kinda starring at the girl and the girl notices it and asks Frenchy what the hell you lookin at.

Frenchy just turns the other way because she knows that this bitch is crazy. So the girl starts up on Frenchy.

"That's what's wrong, all these uppity hoes thank they shit don't stank and these stupid ass men kiss they ass" she says to her girlfriend aloud so Frenchy can here her.

The girl keeps on and before not too long, Frenchy turns and looks at her like bitch please.

The girl is lookin at Frenchy now and she is looking back at the girl.

"What you lookin at bitch" the girl ask Frenchy.

Frenchy gets up and says "I got you bitch, ugly ass stank hoe. What's wrong you cant keep a man with you pitiful ass".

The girl starts to make her way over to Frenchy and all of the sudden just when she gets in the reach of her, Frenchy slaps her in the head with a glass and knocks her ass out cold right to the floor.

Then she stands there and dust her hands off like it was no problem at all.

Good walks up, grabs her by the arm and tells her "I see you know how to handle your's".

"You danm right I can handle mine. That bitch was talking shit for about ten minutes and I couldn't take no more from that stupid hoe. I aint no easy win" she tells Good.

So Good takes her into the back room and Big comes and gets the girl up and takes her outside and her friend tells Big what had happened.

"That bitch is crazy. She was talking shit to us and all of the sudden she cracks my home girl in the head with a glass".

Big knows the likes of these ghetto hoes because they have started trouble before and so he kicks them out of the club.

He thinks to himself "that's what she gets".

He goes back into the club and goes to the room where Frenchy and Good is.

He walks in and looks at Good and asks him what happened.

Frenchy starts to defend herself telling them both about how that bitch was jealous and going on and on about how I thought I was the shit and I think I'm cute and was calling me out of my name and I just had enough of that hoe so I told that hoe that it's her problem that she cant keep a man. And when she came at me, I clobbered her ass in the head with a glass.

Good and Big both start laughing it up and rolling on the floor because Frenchy knows how to handle hers and that girl was a lot bigger than Frenchy too.

"You go girl" Big tells her. She just smiles at them both and laughs.

Good tells her to just stay in here for a while till things calm down a little bit. So she tells him o.k.

Good tells Big to come back in after about fifteen minutes and keep Frenchy company in the club for awhile. He agrees and goes back to the front door.

The two girls are still out there and start talking shit to Big about Frenchy.

"That bitch better not come out here. I'm gone kick that bitch's ass. I'm gonna fuck that bitch up".

Big looks at them both and tells them "You both better leave right now or there is going to be a problem with me. Yall don't want no problem with me".

They shut up and look at each other and decide that its time to leave. They definitely don't want no problems with Big.

Big is known to crush you with his bare hands and can throw someone all the way across the street.

One time Big had a fight with five dudes at one time and kicked all five of there asses.

So he watches the girls drive off and tells another guy at the door to make sure they don't come back in tonight. Big goes back inside and gets Frenchy out of the back room.

Frenchy is looking around like she is really paranoid because she don't know anyone in L.A. just Good. Big takes her over to the VIP section and they have a seat. Big waves down a waitress and tells her to bring some Champaign over for them.

As they wait on the Champaign, Frenchy starts to wind down.

"So Big, I want to thank you for keeping me company tonight" she tells him.

"Not a problem miss lady" he answers.

"I never had a body guard before" she says.

"Well I never been around someone so fine as you. So where even" he tells her and she gives him a great big pretty smile.

The waitress comes back with the drinks and they give a toast to friends.

"To Friendships" as they hold up there glasses and then sip on the Champaign.

Frenchy gets kinda tipsy after a minute and she tells Big "You know your kinda cute and I never been attracted to a large man before".

Just then Good walks up and says "Everything good over here"? Big nods his head up and down as to say yes.

Good then tells Big "thanks man, I'll take it from here when he notices that Frenchy is kinda tipsy. Big gets up and tells Frenchy to have a good night and it was a pleasure spending this time with you. Then he turns and walks away.

"You alright baby" Good asks Frenchy. He can tell that she has had maybe one to many drinks. She tells him "I'm fine" in a slurred speech.

"I think its time to take you home" he tells her.

"Come on baby, lets go home then" she answers back to Good.

Chapter Seven

Its about twelve midnight and Hound walks into the club. He goes over to the bar to get him a drink and he sees Good walking with his arm around Frenchy. He also sees she isn't walking straight and that she is drunk.

He gets up quickly and walks over to short cut them off.

"Hey Good, what's happening man and what you got here" he says to them.

"Hi Hound" Frenchy says out loud excitedly.

"She's had a little too much to drink" Good answers.

"Hey, you want me to take her back to her hotel. I know were it is and you know you gotta close your club and count all that money" he says in a condescending way.

"You know someone got you for some of your chips one time before" he adds.

"All right man, you can take her. I trust that you won't try to take advantage of her or anything like that, right". Good tells him.

"You got my word man" and Hound takes over putting his arm around Frenchy and guides her to his car outside.

They get out to the car and Big is watching as Hound gets her into the car and closes the door.

Big thinks to himself "I don't like that fool" as he watches them drive off.

Hound and Frenchy get to the hotel soon then he helps her out of the car and into the hotel.

As they both pass the front desk, the clerk asks if everything is all right.

"Yhea, everything is o.k. just a little too much to drink" Hound tells her.

So they get inside the elevator and go up to her floor. Then he gets her outside of her room door.

She finally gets out her room key after a few minutes of looking in her purse for it and they open the door.

He walks her inside and over the bed, then he puts her on the bed and she reaches out and grabs him then tells him to please don't leave her, she doesn't want to be alone tonight.

He tells her that he really didn't plan on leaving her all alone.

She starts telling Hound all about how she had got into a fight in the club and the bitch really got what she deserved. Hound is just listening not really understanding what she is trying to say to him.

"You had a fight in the club" he asks her.

"Yhea, I told you. I had a fight in the club" she answers.

Hound is starting to take off her clothes and undress her as she tells him to make love to her pulling on him and grabbing his pants.

"I dreamed of this" she tells him.

"I dreamed of you too baby" he tells her.

She pulls off his shirt with some help from him and he finishes pulling off her clothes.

There she lies looking sexy and all his for the taking. He starts to kiss her and she kisses him back. He kisses her on the neck and she sucks on his ear lobes. He slides his pants off and then her bra comes off. She's grabbing his penis as if she cant wait and so off comes her panties.

Hound starts to tickle her nipples with his tongue one at a time and lick around her areolas. She loves it because she tells him so.

She tells him to give it to her and she wants it now.

"All right baby, I'll give it to you" he tells her softly in her ear.

He eases up to her pretty face and kisses her in the lips. He slides his hands into her inner thighs to part her legs. Then he lifts her legs up and points his ass in the air ready to slide inside of her.

Hound feels her warm wanting vagina and parts her wet lips with his fingers. Then he slides his hard erect penis into her warm opening as she moans in ecstasy.

"Ooh, yhea baby" she sighs softly into his ear.

Hound slides slowly in and out of her tight little vagina and grabs her ass with two hands from behind. He squeezes her ass as he strokes her a little faster. His hands moving up her outer thigh and down, almost to her ankle as he stokes her a little faster and then he stops his hands at her ass and squeezes her cheeks firmly again.

"That's right daddy, it feels good" she tells him.

"Fuck me harder" she says.

Hound then starts to really put in some work and pump her harder on every second stroke.

Push, pull, thrust. Push, pull, thrust.

"Oh, ah, yhea, oh, ah, yhea" she starts to get louder and louder.

"That's right daddy. Work it" she tells him.

"You like it" he asks her

"Yes baby, ooh, shit" she answers back.

"Uh huh" he tells her every time he strokes and pumps her forcefully.

"Yes baby, yes baby, yes baby" she starts to scream and Hound starts to really give it to her good.

"No baby, no baby, no" as Hound shoves it in all the way deep as if he is trying to knock another hole in it.

Frenchy starts to scream louder and louder and that only makes Hound punish her more and more.

Hound starts to tell her on every stroke about his ego.

"I, aint, no, easy, win" he tells her one word at a time as he strokes her.

"Ewwww" is all that Frenchy can say at this time.

"Eeewwwww" she starts to sound like she's crying.

"Take that" he pounds her stroke by stroke.

This goes on for another few minutes and it seems like for ever to Frenchy.

Every stroke is like so painfully good that she Cums about three or four times during all this.

Hound builds up his climax finally and tells her "I'm Cumming, I'm Cumming" then he pulls out and shoots a great big nut all over her stomach.

"Oh yhea baby" he tells her as he rubs his penis on her stomach in all his semen.

Frenchy lies there squirming and moaning on the bed until Hound is done nuting and rubbing it on her.

He gets up and stands there for a moment and just looks at Frenchy. She is also lying there watching Hound and they just gaze at each others eyes.

"Danm baby, that was the shit" he tells her.

She smiles at him and says "You like that don't you".

He just agrees by nodding his head and turns as he goes into the bathroom.

In the bathroom he looks into the mirror as he turns on the warm water. He gives himself a nod of accomplishment and a smile, while he washes out a face clothe.

"Oh" he moans as he wraps the warm wet towel around his still sensitive erect penis.

He finishes washing him self and goes back into the bedroom only to find Frenchy fast asleep.

He pulls the covers over her, slides into the bed next to her and soon falls asleep himself.

The next morning they both wake up and the sun seems to be shining a little brighter than usual. They both have this glow about them and they can't seem to stop smiling at each other.

"Good morning" Hound tells Frenchy.

"Good morning" she answers back.

"I sure am hungry" Hound says to her.

"I'm starving" she replies.

"You want to order some room service or would you rather go out and get something" he asks her.

"We can order room service, I have a hangover I think" she tells him.

Hound just looks at her and laughs as this he can tell.

"You drank that much last night" he asks her sounding curious.

"Yhea I guess I did" she tells him.

Hound grabs the in room menu and looks at it.

"Hey, I want some pancakes, bacon and eggs" he shouts in excitement.

"Why you gotta holler" she asks him.

"Yhea, get me the same, with some extra syrup and milk" she adds.

"All right baby. Breakfast commin right up" he tells her and calls room service to place there order.

So they spend the rest of the morning enjoying each others company and getting to know more about each other. Hound loves her company and she loves his also. They are a couple of peas in a pod.

"So Hound, when do you think I can come back and see you again" she asks.

"I was thinking that you could come back tomorrow" he tells her.

"Are you serious" she asks him as she looks at him with a big bright smile on her face.

"I tell you what. You call me when you make it back safe and then we will figure out something about you coming back to Los Angeles" he says to her with a twinkle in his eye.

She just smiles at him because she knows that he is really serious about it.

Hound takes her to the airport later on that morning and drops her off at curbside with a skycap to check in.

He gives her a kiss and tells her to make sure she calls him when she makes it back safely. She agrees and gets her purse out of the car and then wave's goodbye as Hound pulls off into airport traffic.

So she gets her ticket and the skycap takes her bag and places it on a cart with some other bags. He tells her not to worry and he was going to make sure her bag gets to where she is going on time.

So Frenchy goes inside and gets through the security checkpoint and lands herself at her gate. She pulls out a magazine and sits there waiting to board the plane for New Orleans.

So Frenchy flys back to New Orleans and when she arrives at the airport Dirt is already waiting there for her.

He walks up to her and gives her a hug and then asks her how her flight was. She answers back it was fine.

They walk over to the carrousel to wait for her bag to arrive and he asks her you didn't have any problems did you. She answers him with a no.

He asks her if she missed him and he tells her that he missed her. She just looks at him like yhea, sure you did.

She realizes that there is a whole world out there and she has had a lil taste of what it has to offer her.

So the bag comes down the shoot and they grab it quickly. They walk out of the baggage claim area and Dirt tells her that the car is this way as he crosses the street first.

They reach the car and Dirt opens the trunk and puts her bag inside. Then he closes the trunk and they walk around the car to get in. She realizes again that he never and probably never will open the car door for her.

She closes the door after she gets in and puts her seat belt on. Dirt starts the car up and they both drive off.

They get away from the airport and Dirt drives straight to his place so he can look at the dope in her bag.

They pull up at his place and park the car. They both get out and head inside with her bag from the trunk.

They reach the front door and he unlocks the door with his key then they both go inside. "Shut the door behind you and make sure that its locked" he tells her.

So she comes inside and then she locks the door behind her.

Dirt puts the bag on the table and opens it up. He digs out the dope and puts it on the side of the table and then puts his hands back into the bag and pulls out some of her underwear. He holds up a sexy camisole and says "I aint neva seen dis befo".

"I bought that in L.A." she immediately replies as he looks at her with the devil in his eyes.

"Looks like you had mo than fun in L.A." he tells her as he swings her underwear back and forth.

He puts the camisole back into the bag and goes over to the dope and tells her "Don't get it twisted, this is about business and nothing else. Don't get side tracked with dem fools out there".

She looks at Dirt thinking if you only knew but answers "Don't worry".

So Dirt walks over to her and tells her "You did a good job baby" as he kisses her. Then her cell phone rings and she tries to ignore it.

Dirt looks at her and asks her if she's going to answer it. She knows that it is probably Hound because she told him that she would let him know when she landed and made it back safely.

The phone stops ringing and soon she gets a tone that there is a message.

Dirt looks at her knowing that it was probably some guy she met in L.A. and says "So, you met someone out in L.A. huh".

She looks at him is silence and doesn't respond. He looks at her and tells her "That's o.k. you don't have to say anything, I aint no fool and I sho wasn't born yesterday".

He snatches the phone from her and looks at it and sees Hound's name on the phone.

She quickly tells him that he is just making sure that she mad it back safely. He looks at her and says "Yhea right, and I'm boo boo the fool".

He walks over to the window, turns around and ask her "Did you fuck him"?

Her eyes light up and she answers back "Hell no".

Dirt pauses for a minute and asks her again "Did you fuck him"?

She looks at him and says louder "Hell No!"

So Dirt walks over to her and tells her that she better not. All Hound is about is his money and he don't care about nobody. She looks at him and thinks to herself, "Yhea, just like you".

She then tells him "I have to check on my mama. Can you take me home?"

He looks at her and says "Yhea, I'll call you a cab. I got some work to do" as he goes over to the dope and touches it.

So she picks up the TV remote and turns it on and changes the channel to some girlie movie. Dirt starts working with the dope, breaking it down and dividing it up. Frenchy gets up and goes into the restroom and sits down on the toilet and checks her message.

"Hey Frenchy, this is Hound. I'm just checking to see if you made it back safe. Give me a call when ever you can. I miss you already. Bye." She hurries and erases the message.

As she sits there thinking of Hound she also thinks about Goodnight.

Goodnight's club was off the hook and he really has it going on. Handsome, smart, tall, talented and he's paid. Two birds with one stone. She flushes the toilet and turns on the sink, looks into the mirror and smiles at herself and gives herself a wink.

"You on your way girl" she tells herself.

She walks out of the bathroom and goes back to the couch and sits down. She stares at the television thinking of her time in Los Angeles and then she hears a car horn outside.

"There's you cab" Dirt tells her.

She gets up and grabs her bag then heads for the door. Dirt tells her "Hey I don't get a goodbye kiss".

She turns around and walks over to him and gives him a kiss on the cheek. Then he pulls out some money and gives it to her for the cab. He also gives her another thousand dollars for her work that she did. She takes the money and puts it away quickly.

"I'll see you later" she tells him as she walks out the door.

Dirt looks out of the window while she gets into the cab and sees her take her phone out as she is getting inside the cab. He thinks to himself "She couldn't wait to get inside the damn cab to call that nigga".

Inside the cab, on her way home, Frenchy calls Hound up on her phone. Hound answers his phone "Hello".

"Hi" she says sounding excited. Hound knows exactly who it is.

"I thought you were going to call me and let me know that you made it safe" he asks her.

"I was going to but I ran into some delays" she tells him.

"Who, Dirt" he asks. "I know that yall got something going on. Don't forget that I except you no matter what" he tells her.

"O.K. babe. I understand. Thanks" she tells him.

"So when can you come back out here? I'll pay for everything, you don't have to worry about nothing" he says.

"When do you want me to come back out" she asks him.

"I can put you on a plane tomorrow, don't think I won't". He tells her.

She knows that he is serious and this is her chance to come up and get away from Dirt.

"How long you want me out there" she asks him.

"Forever" he tells her. "I want you to be my lady and stay with me" he adds.

She thinks about it for a second and tells him that she has to talk to her mother. She is the only one taking care of her mother right now and she has to make sure that her mother is going to be taken care of.

He tells her that it is not a problem and to do what ever she has to do.

"I'll call you back later then" she tells him and they say there goodbyes and hang up.

As the cab pulls up to her mothers place, she looks at the meter and hands the cab driver some money to pay for the cab. She gets out of the cab, grabs her bag and goes into the house.

Chapter Eight

Inside the house she calls out to her mother "Mama, I'm home".

"Baby, is that you. I didn't hear you come in" her mother tells her.

"So tell me all about your big trip to the big city" she tells Frenchy.

"Well mama, I saw some celebrities and everyone has really nice things like cars and jewelry and they all wear designer clothes. Here I got you something mama" as she pulls out a T-shirt that reads Los Angeles and hands it over to her mama.

"Oh, thank you baby" her mama tells her and gives her a great big kiss on the cheek.

"Mama, I have something to talk to you about. I met this really nice man out there and he's really handsome and I like him a lot" before she could finish her mother cuts her off and says.

"Now baby you have to see things clear and don't let money and looks cloud your judgment. You have to be careful that he's not just here today and gone tomorrow. You have to make sure that you really like him for what's inside and not what's on the outside. In your later years when yall are not so beautiful, what will you have and money aint everything you know".

"I know mama, I really like him and for right now he can help me get back into school" she tells her mother.

"Well you have your own life to live baby. Just remember that I love you very much and please be careful".

"So I was thinking about moving out there and I wanted to make sure that you had someone to take care of you while I was gone" Frenchy tells her.

"Your Aunt Lucy and cousin Betty can come check on me from time to time. Don't you worry about me baby, I'll be fine." she says.

"I may leave to go back tomorrow". Frenchy tells her. "He wants me to come back out there and live together."

"I'll call your aunt and cousin and you go live your life girl" her mama tells her.

She goes into the back room and calls up Hound on the phone.

"Hello" he answers.

"Hi, its me" she says sounding excited.

"I talked to mama and we worked out a way for her to be taken care of so I can come back to L.A." she tells him.

"That's great, so I'll check on the flights and book the ticket right now. I'll let you know what flight it is so get ready and I'll call you back" Hound tells her.

"O.K." she answers and hangs up the phone.

Then she starts to pack up some clothes and things to take with her back to Los Angeles. She looks around the room and grabs some shoes, shirts and jeans. Then she goes into the bathroom and gets some of her toiletries. She grabs some perfumes, creams and some lotions and puts them all into her bag.

Then she goes and starts to put some socks and underwear into her bag. She stands there and thinks what am I forgetting. I know I'm forgetting something as she looks around the room. She notices a jewelry box and takes some of her jewelry and tosses into the bag.

"That outa do it" she tells herself and zips the suitcase close.

Later on Hound calls her right back and tells her that she is on the twelve noon flight out of New Orleans and he will be waiting for her when she gets back to L.A.

She tells him that she is so excited and she cant wait to get back to see him.

"So I'll see you tomorrow" he tells her and says goodbye.

"Bye baby" she says and hangs up the phone.

Later that night Dirt calls her up just to say hello and she tells him that she is going out of town for awhile and she doesn't know when she will be back.

Dirt is furious and tells her that they have some more business to finish. She tells him that she will be back to finish there business and not to worry. He tells her to make sure she comes bake soon because I'm gone need you soon. He tells her that this shit aint gone last forever and I'm gone need some more.

"You better have yo ass back by the weekend" he tells her in a threatening tone.

"Maybe I will, maybe I wont" she tells him back.

They go on to argue back and forth for a while and Dirt tells her don't make me kick yo ass bitch. I don't play with my money hoe. Don't make me come lookin for yo ass.

"You aint shit Dirt" she tells him.

"And I aint scared of you. You may punk all these fools around the neighborhood but you don't scare me. I bet you wont run up to a real man, cause he would wup yo ass."

Dirt laughs on the other end of the phone and Frenchy just hangs up. Dirt waits for a minute to call back and then he calls back and tells her that he is sorry and he didn't mean to talk crazy to her.

"You know I'm about my paper and I just got a little razzle dazzled." they both start to laugh.

"You go ahead and do what you gotta do and I'll see you when you get back" he tells her.

"All right then" she answers back and says goodbye.

So Frenchy goes on the rest of the night thinking off and on about Hound and Los Angeles then eventually falls asleep and dreams about the so called good life.

Fast cars, movie stars and more money than a sucka could eva spend. Then all of a sudden she sees fire and a explosion and wakes up almost screaming and very scared.

She sits up and looks out of the window and tells herself that it was just a dream. She calms back down after awhile and falls back asleep.

In the morning she wakes and smells some good food, so she gets up and follows her nose to the kitchen where her mother has cooked a great big breakfast for her. She's got grits, bacon, eggs, pancakes and smothered potatoes.

"Dang mama, you cooked all this" she says to her mother.

"Yhea baby, I thought you might be hungry and I wanted you to travel on a full stomach" she tells Frenchy.

So they grab there plates and start to load up on some good eatin.

"I cant wait to dig in mama" she tells her mama.

"I'm gone miss this while I'm gone" she says.

Her mama tells her "this is how you need to cook for your man in order to keep him. A way to a mans heart is through his stomach baby.

Frenchy looks at her and says "I'll remember that mama" and smiles at her.

So they finish there breakfast and Frenchy helps her clear the table and washes all the dishes as her mama puts the left over's in the refrigerator.

After the kitchen is all cleaned up the both go into the living room and sit on the couch to watch a little T.V. They change the channel to the news and stop there.

"Lets see what kinda nonsense is going on in da world today" her mama says to her.

The TV says that there was a drive bye shooting in the projects' last night and two people were killed. They also go on to mention that it was drug related and that if anyone has any information on the killings please contact the police department.

"This place is getting worse and worse baby" Frenchy's mama tells her. "Maybe its for the better that you getting out of here".

"L.A. aint all that mama, they got gangs and drugs too" Frenchy replies.

"Well, I'm glad you know the difference from right and wrong baby" her mama tells her.

"You did a good job on me mama. You aint raised no fool here" Frenchy says.

Frenchy's mama grabs the remote and changes the channel. She stops at a comedy channel and they watch something a little more not so depressing. They sit and laugh and chit chat and as time goes by Frenchy says "Oh, its time for me to get ready to leave".

She makes her final touches and counts her money and gives her mother two hundred dollars.

"Here mama, this is for you and don't spend it all at one time".

Her mama takes the money and tells her that two hundred dollars can stretch a long time if you make it as she puts it inside her bra.

Frenchy gives her a kiss on her forehead and calls a cab to come get her and take her to the airport.

The cab pulls up shortly and Frenchy gives her mama a big hug and another kiss and tells her that she will call and check on her and not to worry she will be fine.

"Love you Mama" she tells her one last time before she leaves.

She exit's through the front door and out to the cab. The cabby puts her bag into the trunk and they drive off to the airport.

When they reach the airport Frenchy gives him a big tip and he gets out and gets her bag for her and places it out on the curb next to the skycap.

The cab drives off and the skycap checks her in and hands her a boarding pass. The skycap then tells her to go right in and go upstairs to her gate.

So Frenchy gets on the plane and heads back to Los Angeles to meet Hound and see just what he has in store for her.

She reaches L.A. and the weather is so very nice. Where talking about a warm eighty five degrees and not a cloud in the blue sky.

As she gets off the plane and walks to her arrival carousel she calls up Hound.

"Hey baby" she says to Hound.

"Hey honey" he answers back to her.

"I just landed, and thought I'd call you" she says.

"I'll be there in a few minutes o.k." he tells her and then they both hang up there phones.

Frenchy waits patiently and her bag finally comes out of the carousel shoot. She grabs her bag, checks the tag to make sure it's her bag and heads for the door.

She goes outside and waits by a bench. She is too excited to sit down and after about ten minutes, then she finally sits down on the bench.

Her cell phone rings and its Hound.

"Hey baby, what terminal you at" he asks her.

"I'm at terminal four" she tells him.

"I'm coming around the airport right now. I'll be there in a minute" he says.

"You're on the lower level, right" he asks.

"Yhea baby, that's right" she answers.

So she sees Hound bend the curve and she stands up. She waves at him and he flashes his head lights so she knows he sees her. She turns around to grab her bag and Hound pulls up to her, jumps out and gives her a great big giant hug.

"There's my baby" he says just before he hugs her.

"Did you miss me" Frenchy asks him.

"I sure did baby" he says.

He puts her bag into the car and closes the trunk then he opens the door for her. She gets in and he closes the door, walks around to the other side and gets inside the car.

So they pull off and Hound tells her "You aint stayin at no Hotel this time, you comin to my place". Frenchy's face lights up and she gets a little excited.

"So where do you live" she asks Hound.

"I live in Brentwood" he tells her. "It's just next to Westwood, right down the four o five freeway".

"Close to the beach" she asks.

"Not too far from the beach. Santa Monica beach is about ten or fifteen minutes away from us" he says.

She notices that he said us and not me. So she thinks that he is starting to count her in as a couple.

"Us as in me and you" she asks him.

"Yhea, me and you as in the two of us" he answers her.

So Frenchy and Hound continue to talk and then he tells her "have I ever told you a joke about the three vampires in the bar".

"No" she answers.

So he starts to tell her the joke.

"O.K. So these three vampires walk into this bar and the bartender sees them come in and says "don't trip, I got this". They come and sit at the bar and he looks at the first one and says "So what will you have buddy". The first one says "I'll have a blood and rum".

He fixes the blood and rum and slides it down to him and looks at the second one.

"And what will you have buddy" he asks him.

"I'll have a blood and coke" the second one says.

So he fixes the second one a blood and coke and slides it down to him. Looks at the third one and says "and what will you have".

The third one says "I'll have a glass of hot water".

So he fixes the hot water and gives it to him and says "excuse me for asking, but what the hell kinda drink is that"?

The vampire pulls out a used tampon and says "I'm going to have tea".

Frenchy starts laughing and cringing at the same time and tells Hound that she has never heard such a gross joke in her life.

"That is just nasty" she adds and Hound is just laughing it up.

"You got any more" she asks him.

"I'll think of some more later" he answers her.

So they pull of the freeway and he asks her is she hungry. She tells him that she is kinda hungry and so they stop and get something.

"Have you ever had a fish taco" he asks her.

"No, but that sounds like it could be good" she tells him.

So they pull up at Wahoo's and order some fish taco's and soda. Later they get to Hounds place and she loves his place alot.

"Wow, this is really nice here and we aint even inside yet" she says.

"Yhea, I like it over here. It's quiet and I don't have no hood elements over here" he says.

"What do you mean" she asks him.

"Well you know. Gangbangers, bums, loud ass hoes with drama, crack heads, I could go on and on" he tells her.

"Wow, that's all I've been around all my life" she says and adds "So It's pretty boring here" and starts laughing.

"I like boring" he tells her. "My own homies in my old neighbor hood tried to set me up and jack me. That's when I knew it was time to get the hell out of there".

"People will hurt you if they just think that you have something of value. Times is hard enough so I moved over hear but I had to think smart about it.

I know that these white folks would not want some dope dealer living in there hood so I act like I work and get up and come back every day like I have a regular job. I even dress the part. No saggin jeans and white t-shirts for me".

Frenchy starts bustin up laughin and says to him "You seem to really have your shit together".

"Thought you knew" he tells her. "So now all I need is a good woman on my team" he says with a smile on his face.

"I would like to be that woman for you" she tells him. "I want to go to school and get me a degree so I can get me a real good job".

"Well, I can pay for your school if you're really serious" he tells her.

"You would do that for me" she asks him.

"Yhea, sure, if you're my woman, I would do that" he answers her.

She grabs him and gives him a great big hug and a kiss right in the mouth.

So Frenchy moves in with Hound and he pays for her school. She keeps in touch with her mother and tells her everything about what's going one with her new man.

Meanwhile back in New Orleans, Dirt knows that Frenchy is gone for good and he misses her dearly but still faces that she is not coming back any time soon.

He is not very happy about it at all either. She won't answer his calls, messages or text and then she changed her number.

Dirt feels like he got played and the talk in the hood don't help it none neither. Dirt busted one guys face open just because he was saying that Frenchy left Dirt for some L.A. Player.

One of her home girls Lady, still keeps in touch with her, she knows everything and Dirt knows it. So one day before the holidays came he figured that she might come home for the holiday to see and be with her mama.

He had someone play Lady into slipping and telling them that she was definitely going to be coming home for the holiday.

So he set up a little plan.

Frenchy came home for Thanksgiving, had the holiday with her mama and Dirt had someone watching her. She stayed for two days and when she left to go back he had her followed and even had someone in L.A. follow her back to her home in Brentwood.

So now Dirt knows where she stays and even had a picture of who she was with. Hound.

"That no good, snake ass, knife stabbin me in the back mutt" he shouts angrily. "He takes my girl and plays with my mutha fuckin money".

Dirt thinks back and figures it all out. He starts to think about why Hound had acted like he was dumb and why he was saying that it was real dry out there for him and he didn't have any more dope.

"That fool ass been playin me all this time. I'm gone kill that bitch ass nigga" he says.

So Frenchy is very much in love with Hound and he is in love with her. Goodnight accepts that they are in love and steps to the side because he knows that he did have his moment and he will always have a place in his heart for her.

Chapter Nine

Frenchy graduates from college right after Thanksgiving and right before Christmas then someone that Dirt knows, runs into her at her beauty shop.

Dirt finds out where her beauty shop is and goes out to L.A. and waits for her to come out of the shop one day then walks up to her and says "Hey baby, how you doin".

Frenchy turns around, looks at Dirt and almost jumps out of her vanilla skin.

"How you doin baby" he asks her again. "You didn't think you'd ever see me again did you".

She just looks at him in shock and finally says "No, I didn't".

"So you wanna go somewhere and talk or should I tell you how I really feel right here, right now" he tells her as he shows her a gun in his waistband.

She looks him right in the eyes and sees that he is not playing, not one bit. So she tells him "Let's go to my car".

They walk over to her car slowly without saying a word and then they both get inside the car. Dirt sits there and tells her that he knows all about Hound and he doesn't know where they went wrong.

"Why did you leave me" he asks her.

"I don't have a reason" she tells him.

"I know why" he says. He looks at her newly done hair and says "It was the money wasn't it"?

She looks at him and then she shakes her head up and down yes.

"Hound has money and he stole you from me" he adds.

"You know that I really love you baby. I still love you after all this bull shit" he tells her.

"I want to take you back home with me. Do you want to come home with me" he asks her.

She looks at him and just shakes her head no.

"I have a new life out here Dirt. What we had was then and what me and Hound have is now" she says.

"I could come home with you but it wouldn't be the same. I love Hound and he has my heart" she tells him.

"Well maybe I'll just have to take of that" he tells her as he pulls the gun out of his waist.

Frenchy knows that he means business and that Hound is in big trouble now, so she tells Dirt that if she comes home to New Orleans would that settle things. Dirt tells her hell no.

"That fool done played with my money and my emotions plus he took what was rightfully mine. My lady" he says in a angry serious way.

By now Frenchy knows that Hound is in for it and there is nothing that she can do but warn him. She begs Dirt not to harm him but Dirt has his mind made up already and knows that he means it.

He looks at Frenchy and asks her "So now you know, what you gone do"?

She thinks to herself "I got to warn Hound". She starts to get all emotional and starts crying.

"Get the hell out of my car" she tells Dirt.

"Get out now" she screams louder at him.

Dirt gets out of the car and she starts it up and speeds off to get away from Dirt as fast as possible.

He just stands there and watches her leave quickly.

Frenchy gets home and goes into the house. Hound looks at her and he can tell that something is very wrong with Frenchy.

"What is the matter babe" he asks her.

"Dirt" she tells him. "Dirt is here in L.A.".

He looks at her and tells her "I knew this day would come sooner or later baby".

"He said that he was going to kill you" she tells Hound.

"Shit, I aint worried about Dirt baby. I can protect myself" he says as he goes into the drawer and pulls out a hand gun.

"Oh Lord" she blurts out loud.

"Don't worry honey. I have to protect everything I love and that includes you" he says.

"Maybe I should just go back to New Orleans" she says.

"Hell to the no baby. You aint goin no where" he tells her.

Hound then tells her don't worry babe, I'm gonna handle this right now and pulls out his cell phone. He calls up one of his homies and tells him everything.

"There someone I want you to take care of my nigga" he tells his homie.

"I'm gonna come through right now and tell you everything and I'm gonna need a throw away gun too".

His homeboy tells him "I got you man and I will see you when you get here. You still know how to get here right".

"Yhea, I'll come through the canyon" he tells his homie.

"So I'll see you in a minute" his homie says and hangs up the phone.

Hound looks at Frenchy and tells her that he has to go make a run and he will be right back in a little while.

Frenchy doesn't want Hound to go and tells him so.

"I have a bad feeling baby. Don't go" she tells him.

"I'll be right back baby. Don't worry" he says and starts for the door.

"No baby" she says while she tries to get in his way.

"I'll be o.k. baby. I'll be right back" he tells her and walks out of the door.

Hound gets into his car and takes off for the valley. Little does he know that someone is following him. Dirt has followed Frenchy home and is now following him as they head down Pacific Coast Hwy.

Hound is driving kind of fast down PCH and notices in his rear view mirror that someone is following him. So when he gets to Topanga Canyon Blvd he whips a hard right and steps on it.

Dirt banks a hard right after him and the chase is on. Hound gets up to about sixty five miles per hour but has to back off because of all the turns and twist in the canyon. He looks into his rear view mirror and doesn't see Dirt.

After a minute of some more hair pin turns he sees Dirt in the mirror so he smashes the gas pedal.

Dirt is catching up slowly but surely and after a second he catches up to Hound because of a car in front of him blocks him from going any faster.

They get to a curve with a cliff and Dirt tries to get on the side of him and backs off because of a car coming on the other side right at him.

Another turn comes up and Dirt tries to get on the side of him again and this time with his window down he shoots a round at Hound and the bullet goes through the driver side window.

Hound smashes the gas and tries to get away but the cars in front of him won't let him get away.

He reaches for his gun and looks in the mirror for Dirt.

Dirt catches back up to him again and this time when he tries to pass him up he pulls up on the side of Hound and just looks at him with a grin on his face.

When Hound looks at him and points his gun at him, Dirt points his gun at Hound and shoots twice then crashes the car into the side of Hound making him drive uncontrollably off the side of the cliff.

The car tumbles deep down the side of the canyon and crashes into the rocks below and then explodes into a ball of fire as it tumbles down even further into the bottom of the canyon.

Dirt drives on and just shouts and laughs about it saying "Got that fool ass mutha fucka. The big payback. Ha ha ha ha haaaaa".

Later on that night, Frenchy starts to wonder because she's not getting a call from Hound saying that he's o.k. and when he'll be home.

So Frenchy calls up Good because he knows some of the same people that Hound knew.

"Hey Good, this is Frenchy. I think something terrible has happened" she tells him franticly.

"What are you talking about" he asks her.

"My ex-boyfriend found out about me and Hound and I think he's killed him" she tells him as she starts to cry on the phone.

"What, why would you say that" he replies.

"Because he is just that crazy and it's a long story. Can you help me? I think he wants to kill me too" she says nervously.

Good is very confused and tells her to meet him at the club right away.

So Frenchy gets herself together and leaves her place in Brentwood looking very paranoid. She peeks out of the door before she walks out and heads for the garage.

When she gets to the garage she peeks in and behind the door and walks quickly to get into her car. She is so nervous that she can barely get the key into the door.

She starts up the car and opens up the garage door. She backs out and heads out of the garage onto to the street.

She looks at all the cars on the street and looks both ways down the street. Nothing seems to be out of place so she punches it down the street and makes her way to the club. She is so nervous that she watched her rear view mirror all the way there.

She gets to the club and before she parks she circles the block just to make sure that no one is following her.

She parks in the rear of the club and gets out and makes her way into the back door without anyone seeing her go in.

"Good" she screams as she enters the club.

"Here I am Frenchy" he answers.

She goes up to him and gives him a great big hug. Terrified for her life she tells Good all about how it all happened and how she thinks that Hound is dead.

"Well first things first" he tells her. "You need to stay at my place till we get things straight. Don't even go home for clothes or nothing because I think he may know where Hound was living".

She looks at him and says "Thank you so much".

Good looks at her and tells her not to worry even though he was worried himself.

This is not the first time that Good had a run in with danger. Being from the streets himself he knows just how killers think and what they might try.

Good gets on the phone and calls up one of his good friends that also knows Hound and asks him if he knows anything about what might have happened. The guy tells him no, he hasn't heard anything.

Good calls up another one of his homies that works with the police department and asks is any thing was reported or found about Hound.

The police officer told Good that there was a strange accident in the Topanga Canyon area and said that he would look into it and let him know more.

So they wait for a few minutes and the cop calls back and tells him that a car was forced off the road and a witness said that shots where fired.

"Do you know who the car was registered too" he asks and the cop tells him that the car was registered to Duwayne Young. Hound's real name.

He tells him thanks man and hangs up the phone. Then he looks at Frenchy and says "Hound is Dead".

She starts to cry and shouts out loud "Noooo".

Good walks over to her and gives her a hug to comfort her.

Then Big walks into the room and sees them hugged up and says "Oh, excuse me you too".

Good says "No, it's all right" and pulls away from Frenchy.

"Man, this sweet lil angel has gotten herself into some serious trouble" he tells Big.

Big stands there, just looking at Good. So because he is no stranger to trouble, and lives for some good drama and danger, he says "Do tell, do tell".

Good lets him know everything about Frenchy and what has happened up until now.

"Don't worry baby, I don't like no country slick ass fools anyway" Big tells her as he pulls out a forty five semi automatic pistol.

"So what does this fool look like" they ask her.

She pulls out her phone and shows them both a few pictures of Dirt.

"That's one ugly nigga" Big tells her.

So they agree that she was not to drive her car. It should stay parked in the back of the club and she should stay away from home.

They both make some phone calls and put the word out that there is a fool out here from New Orleans and he is marked.

So now they try to figure out where she can stay.

Good tells them that his girl is at his place right now so they agree to let her stay at Big's place.

So it's getting really late and they know that they are going to have to lay low until this blows over.

They also know that this fool aint gone give up easy. One thing that you don't mess with is a hustler's money. You can take his bitch but don't mess with his money. So they know that Frenchy is marked and he wont stop till either she is dead or he is.

They get ready to leave the club and go over to Big's place. Good tells Big to pull around back and that he knows how to handle this.

Big parks in the rear of the club and goes back inside to get Frenchy. They say a few more words and tell Good that they will see him tomorrow. Then they leave out the back door of the club and make it inside the car.

Good locks up the club and takes his ass home. Big and Frenchy pull off and go toward Big's place in the hood.

So when Good gets home his lady is acting very nosey about where he has been. So Good tells her everything and all she can say is "poor thing".

When Big and Frenchy get to the hood, Big asks her if she wants anything to eat and she tells him no thanks, she doesn't have an appetite.

So they pull up to the spot and before they get out Big tells her that he doesn't think anyone is crazy enough to follow him and he gets out of the car and tells her come on baby, lets go inside.

So they both walk sort of fast to get inside the house and as they go inside Big locks the door behind them then turns on some light and lights a candle.

He turns and looks at Frenchy and tells her that the candle is for protection.

So Big goes into the kitchen and comes out with some glasses and some wine.

"Here is some Moscato to calm your nerves down a little bit". They poor the wine and chit chat a little bit about Dirt and what he's like. Then Big starts talking about himself and how he put it down back in the day.

After drinking some wine Big turns on some music and starts to dance a little bit. He dances over the where Frenchy is sitting and reaches out to her but she does not respond. He grabs her and tries to pull her up but she still resists to get up and dance.

Big pours her some more Moscato and dances around the place singing and laughing. Frenchy cant help but to start laughing at Big, because he looks so crazy with his terrible dancing and horrible singing.

Big focuses in on her beautiful smile dances his way back over to her. Standing over her, he tells her that she has a very beautiful smile.

At that instant, she realizes that Big may just be her protection from Dirt. She raises her hand up at Big to help her get off the couch.

Big takes her hand and lifts her up and they start to dance together around the room. Round and round, back and forth they glide around with one another to the beat of the music.

Frenchy looks into Big's eyes and tells him "your pretty light on your feet for a big guy".

He just smiles at her as he pulls her a little tighter to him. Frenchy lifts her hands over his broad shoulders, puts her hands on the back of his neck and interlocks her fingers together.

Big can't help it because Frenchy is so fine that he starts to get a little excited and his pants starts to poke out at Frenchy.

She then smiles at Big and tells him "I see someone is getting a little excited".

"I can't help it, you really turn me on" he tells her.

Frenchy takes her hands from around Big's neck and puts one of her hands on his protruding bulge.

"I see why they call you big" she tells him as she squeezes his penis.

Big just stands there in shock and then she guides him over to the couch. She unfastens his belt and unzippes his zipper. She sits on the couch and takes his extra large penis out of his pants.

His pants drop to the floor as she holds his hard erect penis the size of a little baby's arm.

At first she just holds it looking at it as she doesn't exactly know what to do with it because it is so big. Then she starts to lick and kiss on it.

Big starts to moan and groan, telling her that it feels good. So she then tries to put the large head into her small mouth. It almost doesn't fit.

So she just licks on it mostly and stokes him with two hands.

"You want some of this tight pussy" she asks him.

"Yhea lil mama" he answers.

"Tell me you want it" she commands him.

"I want you, I want you so bad" he tells her.

Frenchy now thinks that he will do what ever she wants him too; all she has to do is ask him.

She stands up and takes off her clothes and Big joins her and takes off all his clothes also. There they stand, both naked and horny.

Frenchy tells Big to take her to the bed and Big waste no time picking her up and carrying her into the bedroom. He throws her on the bed and she tells him to be gentle.

She looks up at him and there stands like a giant looking down at her. So he bends down over her and starts to kiss on her.

He kisses her neck, her titties and then stomach all the way down between her thighs. Then he splits her lips with his fingers and licks between her crotch searching for her clit.

"There it is" he says as she starts to squirm like a fish out of water.

Now she knows that they are at the point of no return and Big is really going to give it to her good.

"I want you to kill my ex" she tells him and he stops everything.

"What do you mean" he asks her.

"I want you to kill my ex before he kills me" she tells him.

"I will do anything for you" she adds.

Big tells her o.k. without really thinking it through because she has his dick in her hand at this point and all he wants to do right now is fuck her brains out.

"O.K. fuck me, fuck me now" she begs him.

She takes his hard stiff penis and guides his head to her warm wet opening. She rubs just the head against her wet lips and smears her juices on the tip of his dick.

Then she tries to put it inside but it is too big and wont fit. She opens her legs wider and tells him to slowly ease it in.

He grabs her ankles with both hands, spreads her legs apart and slowly lets her guide his head inside her.

She opens her mouth as wide as she can as if it was helping open her vagina and inside goes the head.

He starts to stroke her slowly with just his head inside her and she starts to moan out loud.

"Oh Big, it's too big" she tells him as she can't believe that he is inside of her tight vagina.

"You're stretching me" she tells him.

This of course only makes him even more excited and harder so he tries to put some more of himself into her small wet pussy.

As he shoves some more of himself inside her she tries to push him away because she can't seem to take it.

He only wants her more and more as she tries to push him back and away.

He slides inside a little more and more every time she pushes him back out of her. She is screaming and shouting at this time because he is so large and she has never experienced anything like this before.

"No" she tells him as he stokes inward.

"Yes" he answers as he pulls out and slides all the way back in.

"Nooo" she cries out sounding like a little girl.

"Yhea baby" he tells her in his sinister voice.

"No, no, no, no, yes, yes, yes, yes" she starts screaming as he starts to stroke her a little faster and faster.

Big is now in full swing, stroking her tight vagina as she begs and pleas for it. She is pulling on his ears and neck uncontrollably.

"Fuck me, fuck me, fuck me" she shouts repeatedly almost hysterical.

Big pounds away in her vagina with no mercy, sliding back and forth in and out of her, stroking and almost pulling her insides out as he withdraws back out of her.

"I'm Cumming" she shouts out loud as she starts patting on the bed and gets her nut all over his hard penis.

"I'm still Cumming" she says as she continues to pat faster and get hers.

"It won't stop, it won't stop" she screams out even louder as she never has experienced anything like this before.

Frenchy can feel his hard penis start to stiffen even harder and knows that he is going to cum soon.

"Cum on baby, cum" she shouts as she slaps him on the ass.

"I'm going to cum baby" Big tells her softly.

"Cum on baby, cum on" she screams.

Big starts to really pound her and then he gives her some long hard powerful strokes.

"Oh, yhea baby, that's it" she screams louder as she is kicking, pulling, slapping and almost fighting him.

"I'm Cumming, I'm Cumming, I'm Cumming" he shouts as he pulls out and shoots his nut all the way up to her pretty little face.

"Ow" she screams unexpectedly.

Big strokes his penis as to ejaculate all over her stomach and smears it around with his dick.

"Yes baby, that's it" she tells him as she lies there feeling used and punished.

Her vagina is really stretched wide open and she can't believe that she just let this big ass dick man do this to her. She can't even move yet so she just lies there for a moment.

Big gets up and goes into the bathroom to clean himself up. When he returns a few minutes later, there she is sound asleep and he just lets her sleep.

Big goes to the other side of the bed and lies there starring at the ceiling for a little while then he passes out himself and falls into a deep sleep.

Chapter Ten

When they wake up in the morning Frenchy can still feel that someone has beat up her tight little vagina and gets up to go into the bathroom to take a bath.

"Good morning" Big tells her.

"Good morning" she answers back.

Big tries to be funny and says "I had a really weird dream that we had sex" and smiles at her.

She looks at him with her sore ass coochy and tells him "I'll never forget it" and smiles back at him.

"You hungry" he asks.

"Yhea, I'm starving" she answers as she seems to have forgotten about Dirt.

"I have some bacon and eggs in the kitchen, can you cook" he asks her.

"Yhea, I can do a little something in the kitchen" she answers.

So Big goes into the front room and sits at the couch with a pencil and pad. Frenchy finishes taking her bath and gets breakfast started.

"What you doin" she asks Big.

"Some thinking about how I'm gone do this" he answers.

"Do what" she says.

"Get rid of your ex" he tells her.

"Dirt, that's right" she remembers.

"So I think that he is probably watching your house or has someone else watching you" he tells her.

"Does he really want to kill you or do you think that he just wants to hurt you" he asks her.

"He had a chance to kill me all ready so maybe he just wants to hurt me" she says.

"Well until we get this all fixed and done with, you can stay here and Good will let you work at the Club" he assures her.

"I'm just so scared. I know that fool is crazy and won't hesitate to trip out" she tells Big.

"Don't worry, I'll protect you" he tells her again.

So they eat breakfast and think of how this might all go down. They think of maybe using Frenchy as bait to lead Dirt to the club first. Then they think of baiting him to a different location and Big tells her that he will come up with something himself.

"I don't want you to know anything about it so you won't be able to say anything if you get caught up with the police and end up taking a lie detector test or something" he tells her.

She just looks at him and realizes that this may not be the first time he has done something like this and all his talk earlier my have just been real talk. She thinks about if this is really what she wants and knows that once it is done that she will have to live with the secret for the rest of her life.

Big sees the look on her face that's saying she is worried so he tells her that from this point on she wont know anything that goes on and if he is even dead or not.

"You will go on with the rest of your life like he never existed" he tells her.

"I don't want you to say or talk to anyone about this. Do you understand? Not even Good" he tells her.

She just nods at him and doesn't even open her mouth.

So a little later Big leaves and tells her before he leaves not to go anywhere and don't even go outside.

Frenchy sits around Big's place and watches some TV for awhile then she tries to read a magazine that Big has on the table.

Good calls her on her phone and tells her that she can help out at the club until things blow over.

Then Big calls her later and asks her what size she wears because he needs to buy her something to wear to the club tonight. She tells him that she wears a size four and he describes the outfit that he is holding up for her in the store.

She agrees that it is something that she might like and they put together something for her.

Later on that day Big comes home with some cheese burgers and finds Frenchy watching TV on the couch.

"Hey, I thought you might be hungry so I brought some cheese burgers" he tells her.

"Thank you big. I'm starving" she replies.

"We gonna leave after a while for the club so you can start getting ready" he says.

"What should I wear" she asks him.

"Wear this sexy outfit" he answers her back as he pulls out what he bought from the store.

So Big goes into the bedroom to start pulling out something for himself to wear tonight at the club. And later Frenchy puts on her sexy outfit.

So they leave after awhile and head for the club. When they get there they pull into the back and park there. They go inside without being seen and they show her where she will be working tonight.

Good tells her that she has to wash glasses in the back kitchen and she doesn't like it but knows that she needs them right now and this is the least that she can do to show her gratitude.

She looks at Big and says "I thought you told me to wear something sexy".

"I didn't know that you were going to be working in the kitchen" and starts laughing at her.

She's stares at him and gives him the evil eye.

"So we know what he looks like if he comes to the club tonight" Good tells her.

"My homie tells me that someone was asking about a cute light skinned honey" he tells Big.

"If he does come here he better make it in through the back door, because he aint gone make it alive through the front door.

So later they open the club and start serving drinks. Frenchy starts to wash some glasses and stuff.

So for a few nights, things don't change and the club goes on as usual.

Then one night out of the blue Dirt makes it passed the front door into the club. He walks around the club for awhile, stops at the bar and orders a drink.

"Can I have a Remy on the rocks" he orders.

"Coming right up" the bar tender says.

He fixes his drink and gives it to him then Dirt asks about Frenchy. The bartender at that moment realizes that this is the guy and gets a little nervous. He tells one of the waiters to go get Good.

Good comes by the bar and the bar tender gives him the high sign and looks at Dirt. Good sees its him and goes to the front door and pulls Big inside and whispers to him that Dirt is inside the club at the bar.

Big gets on the phone and text a couple of his homies so they can lure Dirt out of the club.

Then he goes back outside and tells the other doorman that he will be gone for awhile.

Big sees his homies arrive and he shows them who Dirt is sitting at the bar.

So they go over to the bar and stand next to Dirt and wink at the bartender. Then they say hey can we get a couple of French Connections. The bar tender looks at them and tells them "coming right up".

Dirt looks at them and they look like they aint for no play time.

The bartender brings them there drinks and one of the guys grabs the drink and all of the sudden slams the glass up against Dirt's head. The other guy grabs Dirt and holds him up as the other one starts to punch him in the stomach and then he gives him a right cross and knocks his ass out.

Everything happens so fast that almost no one even sees what has happened except for the ones at the bar.

They drag him out the back door and through him into the back of a SUV with his hands duck taped. They pull off and Big is driving with one car following him.

They arrive at an abandoned warehouse and pull in side. Dirt is awake when they pull him out of the SUV and throw him onto the floor.

Dirt stands there above him telling him that in case you didn't realize it you are not in New Orleans fool.

"This is L.A. fool and I'm gone show you how we do it on the west side" he says.

One of his homies kicks him right in the side and slaps him in the face. The other kicks him again and punches him in the face. They both take turns hitting, punching and kicking on him.

Then Big tells them maybe you guys want to leave now.

"You might not want to see what's going to happen next".

So they leave Big and Dirt by themselves and Big takes the tape off of Dirt and tells him "I'm gone give you a fighting chance".

Dirt slowly stands up and Big punches Dirt in the face knocking him back to the floor. Dirt gets back up slowly and Big punches him again knocking him back down to the floor.

Big tells Dirt to get up and he just lies there.

"I said to get up" Big yells at him again.

Dirt gets up slowly and looks Big in the eyes. Big walks over to him and before Big could hit him again Dirt punches Big in the throat and then kicks him in the nutts. Big falls to his knees on the floor and Dirt gives him a right cross to the chin and then a upper cut that puts him down on the floor.

Dirt stands over him and tells him "You thought I was a easy win didn't you".

Dirt walks over to where Big's gun is and picks it up. Big gets up, runs at Dirt and attacks him and then they struggle for the gun.

Big gets a couple of good ones in but Dirt doesn't let go of the gun then Dirt plays dirty and knees Big right in the crotch again and Big goes down.

Dirt points the gun at Big and fires two shots point blank range, right in the chest area.

Bigs two homies come runnin back inside and start shooting at Dirt so he flees and runs away out the back door and down the alley.

"Big, you all right" one of his homies asks him.

"I been shot you fool" Big tells him "of course I aint all right".

So they get Big up and get him to the hospital where they say that they were caught up in some trouble at the club and someone took a couple of shots at Big.

The cops had to make a police report about it so they lied about everything and said it happened so fast that they really didn't get to see what kind of car or what the guy looked like.

But they know that they have to take care of Dirt.

So the doctor comes out of emergency about an hour later and tells them that Big is very lucky, the bullets went right through and that he will be fine.

They give each other hugs and ask the doctor when they can see him. The doctor tells them that he has to rest and maybe in about six hours.

So the leave the hospital and contact Good. Good tells them to come and take Frenchy to his place and when he closes the club he will be there.

So the two home boys get back to the club and go inside and tell Good all about what happened and how Dirt ended up getting away after shooting Big. Good tells them that you can never under estimate your opponent.

"Big knows better than that" he says looking confused. He sits there and thinks about it for awhile and figures out that Big must have gotten involved with Frenchy and took things personal and wrapped his feelings into business.

Good goes and tells Frenchy that something has gone wrong and that she will have to stay at his place.

"Big is o.k." he says to her and not to worry. She asks what happened and he tells her that Big got shot in the chest but he is o.k.

She starts crying and gives Good a hug and he assures her that everything is going to be all right.

"Come on, my boys are going to take you to my place and I will be there when I close up tonight" he tells her as he grabs her hand and walks her to the room where they are waiting.

He gives one of his homies the keys to his place and tells him to make sure that you are not being followed and don't let anyone else inside. You can leave her there by herself and I will be there in about an hour and a half.

They take the keys and leave out to the car and then they pull off headed to Goods place.

Good gets on the phone and calls up Sticks.

"Hey man, what it do" Sticks says.

"Man, things are going crazy over here and I may need your help" he tells Sticks.

"What ever you need man, you know that I'm there for you" he answers.

"I'll tell you all about it later. I just wanted to let you know that I may need some help" he lets Sticks know.

"Straight man, I'm here" he replies.

"All right, I'll see you later man" Good tells him and they hang up the phone.

So Frenchy gets to Goodnights place and they make it inside without being seen or followed. They drop her off and then they leave.

Good closes up the club and goes home thinking about Frenchy all the way there. There is something on his mind about her that he can just not figure out. Why is so many people getting involved with her and getting hurt.

He makes it home and parks his whip and goes inside the complex. He knocks on the door and says "It's me open the door".

Frenchy comes to the door and looks through the peep hole to see that its Good so she opens the door and lets him in.

Good locks the door behind him and puts his coat on the couch and Frenchy comes over to him and gives him a great big hug. They stand there for a moment and enjoy the hug and then Good tells her to come sit down and that he wants to talk to her.

So they sit on the couch and Good asks her why is it that just about everyone that she comes across is getting hurt. She just looks at him and he asks her if she is cursed or something. And she starts laughing and tells him of course not.

He then asks her if she knows any voodoo or anything like that and she looks at him smiling and tells him no, nothing like that.

"So why is everyone that you come across out here getting hurt or dying" he asks her.

She just looks at him.

"I remember when you first came out here. You got with me and then you got with Hound. Did you just use Hound for his money" he asks her.

"Tell me the truth" he says to her as she just sits there and looks down at the floor.

"I aint mad at you, but just tell me the truth" he says to her.

She looks up at him, shakes her head up and down and tells him yes.

"Yes, I did kinda use Hound but I really loved him. He was really nice to me and made me laugh a lot".

Good looks at her and tells her "I understand".

"He also paid for me to go to school" she says as she wipes the tears from her eyes.

"I'm so sorry that this had to happen. It's all my fault" she cries out.

She looks at Good and tells him "Please help me. I don't want to die and I know that Dirt is going to kill me".

"So you're going to have to lay low for awhile, stay indoors till this settles down and we can take care of things. I won't let Dirt get to you" he tells her.

So Frenchy lays low at Goods place for awhile and the days pass by. Weeks pass by and then she starts to go crazy being inside the house all of the time.

One day she calls up Good and tells him "I can't take this anymore. I can't be locked inside like a caged animal. I have to get out of here".

He tells her that he understands and that she has to remember that its her life that she is playing with.

So Frenchy finally gets out of the house and goes right to the mall to do some shopping. Hound had quite a bit of money stashed away that she had access to and it is all hers now that he is gone.

So she calls Big and asks him how is he doing and he lets her have it.

"So you want to know how I'm doing. I'm doing fine but I don't appreciate you playin me like that. You lead me on to help you with your situation and used me to take care of your dirty work" he tells her.

"No, it wasn't like that at all" she says.

"It was like that and you don't care one bit about me almost dying or nothing" he says angrily.

Frenchy tells him please meet with me. I'm so sorry the way things went but I have been hiding out and Good told me not to use the phone to call no one.

"Is that right" he asks.

"Yhea, that's right and you know the situation already. Meet me somewhere" she asks.

"I'll meet you at the park in Culver City, Fox Hills Park. Do you know where it is?" he asks her.

"No" she replies.

"Then you name the place" he tells her.

"Meet me at the Park and Ride on Crenshaw and the 105 frwy" she tells him.

"I'll be there in twenty minutes" he says.

"I'll see you there" she tells him and hangs up the phone.

So after twenty minutes she meets big at the Park and Ride and she runs up and gives him a great big hug. She tells him that she is so grateful that he helped her out and no one else would never do that for her.

Big is really a softy under his hard appearance so he tells her that its o.k. and he knew that the job was dangerous when he took it.

"I've been shot before you know" he tells her in a joking way. She just looks at him with a serious looks on her face.

Frenchy goes on to tell him that what they had that one night was special and that she really likes him and was not trying to play him at all. Big looks at her and smiles because he actually felt something that night also and thinks it was more than just sexual feelings.

She calls up Good and tells him that she is with Big and they are going to get something to eat together.

"Don't worry, I'll be o.k." she tells him.

Meanwhile Dirt has a connection in Compton that he can go to for assistance when he needs it. He has some guy setup a system that searches for Frenchys phone every thirty minutes and can tell where she uses it. It's only gives him the Longitude and Latitude but he can put that in another program and that will tell him what streets and where about you are or where that call was made.

Chapter Eleven

So Frenchy and Big end up leaving together
and going to get something to eat out in Down
town Disney, Anaheim, CA.

Frenchy leaves her car in the Park and Ride
parking lot and they drive off in Big's car.

Dirt gets a call from his boy in Compton and
he tells him that she used her phone in the last
thirty minutes and it was at Crenshaw and one
hundred and twenty street.

Dirt waste no time and goes right over to
the location where she used her phone hoping
to see her there but he doesn't so he just sits
there for a moment and thinks for a while.

"Why would she be here at the Park and
Ride" he asks himself looking around the
parking lot for any clue.

He sees a couple of people walking around
but doesn't see her so he just sits and wonders,
patiently watching for a sign or clue.

So Big and Frenchy finish eating and then decide to go to a movie together after there delicious, intimate meal together.

After the movie they finally go back to the Park and Ride and as they pull up at the light on the corner of the lot, Dirt gets tired of waiting and drives off the lot to the light.

There they are at the same light and don't even see each other sitting across the street from each other at the same light.

The light turns green so they pass right by each other and Big turns right into the parking lot. They sit there in the car and talk a little bit about where there strange relationship is going and Big knows that she also likes Good so he asks her about Good.

Frenchy calls up Good on the phone and tells him that she has to talk to him and it can't wait. He tells her to come to the club and they can talk there.

Dirt gets a call from his homey in Compton and he tells Dirt that she is using the phone again at the same location.

So Dirt turns around and heads right back to the Park and Ride lot. When he gets there they are gone but he notices that the black Mercedes that was on AMG rims was gone too. He noticed that car from them all because that is the car of his dreams and he really wants that car bad.

He sits in the lot for a moment and waits to see if anything is going to surface but nothing happens.

Good is at the club with Sticks and a couple of other musicians going through some of there material for the weekend coming up when Frenchy arrives there.

"Hey baby" Good greats her.

"These are the fellas" he tells her.

"Hi fellas, my name is Frenchy" she tells them.

"Excuse me for a minute guys, I have to speak to her in private for a moment" he tells them as they walk off into the back room.

They enter the room and Good tells her so what is it that you want to talk about.

"It's us" she tells him.

"Or is there even a us" she says.

"Well Frenchy, I'm glad that you brought that up because that's something that I wanted to talk to you about also" he says.

"Good don't take me wrong, I love you and I appreciate all the things and help that you have given me" she says.

"But what, you're in love with Big" he asks her.

She doesn't say a word she just nods her head up and down. Good walks over to her and asks her if she even knows what love is. She just looks at him for a moment and starts to cry.

Good goes big on her telling her that she really doesn't even know what love is all about and that he has seen her kind before.

"You are lost, always searching and not capable of really loving anyone. You think that you can give your body and that's all that it will take to be loved back. Well your wrong my sister" he tells her.

"I'm trying to help you to my fullest ability and then you come in my club and tell me that you're in love with someone else" he adds.

Frenchy just sits there, looking at him with tears in her eyes.

"Well I hope that my homeboy Hound left you all the money that you can ever want because I see now that you are nothing but a user" he tells her as he points in her face.

Frenchy picks up the phone and calls up Big.

"Big tell Good that I'm not a user and that we are really in love". Then she hands the phone to Good.

Meanwhile Dirt's homey calls him back again and tells him the location of where she is using her phone and he says that the club is at that location.

"Those fools think that I must be really dumb, but I got a surprise for them fools" he tells his homey.

"You need some help dog" his homey asks him and he tells him to meet him at the club with some tools ready to go to work.

"I got you homey. I still owe you dog" his homey tells him and hangs up the phone.

Big tries to explain but Good dosen't want to hear it and hangs up on him.

Big grabs his gun and heads down to the club.

So Frenchy is pouring her heart out at Good, the thugs from Compton are on there way with Dirt and Big is also on his way to the club.

This is a recipe for disaster.

Good knows that Big aint no body to be played with so he calls up some backup from the eastside.

"Yo Baby Two" he says when his homey answers the phone.

"Yhea, who dis" he answers back.

"Dis Good at the club and I needs to see yall at the club with some back up if you know what I mean" he tells him.

"We on the way" he tells Good without wasting any time.

Goods boys are on the way without hesitation and after a few minutes they all arrive almost one after another.

Goods homies get there first and go inside, then Big arrives and also goes inside. Then the guys from Compton show up and Dirt pulls into the lot also.

Dirt see's the same Benz with the AMG rims that he saw at the Park and Ride lot and knows that it must be Frenchy's car.

Inside Big is confronting Good about if he was taken care of business, Frenchy wouldn't be with him and he knows that he's got a lady anyway so what the hell is he mad at in the first place.

Outside Dirt and his crew are loading up there guns for a big surprise and then they start to head for the front door.

Stick's comes inside the back office with his AK47 and asks if everything is all right. Big pulls out his Mac-11 full auto with fifty round drum and then Good pulls out his Glock 18 full auto with 33 round magazine.

Frenchy stands there and starts screaming "No, no please, no" and then all the sudden they hear some noise and a couple of gun shots from the front room and then hear someone shout "I know your in here Frenchy, get ready to meet the devil".

Everyone in the back room looks at each other, and the look on their faces agree that who ever it is in the front room picked the wrong time and place today.

Good's homies look confused so they stand there looking hesitant.

Big then gives a wave of his hands and lets everyone in the room know that he is going out first. Good follows Big and Sticks follows Good out to the front room.

Big shouts as he enters the front room "Start dancing mutha fucka" and shoots at the first thing he sees moving.

His bullets start flying out of his gun so fast that two of the fools didn't even get a chance to see what hit em.

Dirt and a couple of his homies start firing back and then Good and Sticks join right in on the bang bang shoot em up.

Stick's is standing up like he is Scarface or somebody screaming "say hello to my little friend" and damn near shot off one of them fools arm.

Dirt and his homies now know that they better get the hell out of there quick while they still have a chance. So they start to try and run out but Good is pretty handy with his Glock 18 and fires short burst so he can hit his man.

Dirt is cornered in and can't get out so he tells his homie to cover him. When his homeboy starts to try and shoot, Big tears him a new ass hole with his Mac 11 and at that moment Dirt hops his ass out of there like a bat out of hell. Good takes a pop at him while he tries to get out but he misses and Dirt escapes.

Sticks takes off after him yelling "You fuck with me, you fucking with the best".

Dirt jumps into his ride and burns rubber out of there with a quickness but Sticks is right on his ass and fires the AK 47 a couple of times and makes Dirt crash into a pole down the street.

Sticks runs back into the club and tells everyone that he hit that mutha fucka and he crashed into a pole down the street.

Good stands there looking at the fools that came into the club and all the damage that has been done and then he looks at Frenchy like it's all her fault.

Good tells Sticks to get the hell out of there and take the weapons with him.

"Sticks, you're the only one not covered when the police get here. Get the hell out of here".

Sticks agrees by shaking his head up and down and he leaves with Frenchy and they go to his place.

Good and Big go outside and look to see where Dirt had crashed and then they see that the car was down at the corner crashed into a pole.

There was a crowd starting to form and suddenly they hear a scream and see someone get into a car and speed off.

They look at each other and Big say's "I bet that the fool just jacked a car".

"I bet your right" Good answers as he sees Big has been shot.

"Your hit man" Good tells Big.

"It's nothing" he replies.

"I've been shot before and this is nothing. It went right through" he tells Good.

So they go down to the corner and see that Dirt had gotten away but had been shot and was bleeding.

So they go back to the club and when the police arrive they explain that those guys had come into the club and tried to rob them but it was there unlucky day.

We were just getting ready to go to the shooting range and everything just happened so fast.

The cops take some notes and tell the guys that the guys they shot are some known gang bangers and ex felons so that will help them with any trouble that they might have later on.

So the cops wrap up everything at the club and the coroner comes a little later and takes away the bodies.

Good calls up his handy man to come and clean up the place and what a job he has on his hands. There is glass and bullet shells everywhere.

So Good goes over to Stick's place and is very paranoid after the club shoot out. He parks and looks around and gets out and walks up to the door and looks to see if anyone is watching him before he goes inside.

When he goes inside Sticks tells him that if he needs to you can crash out over here.

Good tells him no thanks and that he will be all right at his place. He asks Frenchy is she all right and she looks at him still shaking a little bit and says "Are you serious".

Good can tell that she has never been in a shoot out and she was a total mess.

"Come on lets go home and you can take a bubble bath" Good tells her.

"How did that mutha fucka know that I was in there" she asks Good.

"Maybe he had your phone tracked" he answers her.

"I had my lady's phone tracked and told her where it was when she lost it once" he adds.

Frenchy looks at him like how could she be so lame and let someone do that.

"Why didn't I get a new phone" she asks herself, standing there shaking her head.

Good tells her that he will get her a new phone tomorrow and not to use the other one never ever again.

At that moment she pulls out the battery and throws it away into the trash can.

"Come on, lets go Frenchy" Good tells her.

As they walk over to the door Good tells Sticks thanks for everything and that he owes him big time.

Sticks looks back over to Good and tells him don't mention it and it was nothing as they walk out of the door.

So Good and Frenchy go outside and get into the car and drive off from Sticks place and head for Good's place.

Frenchy is still kinda shaken up and Good tells her that she will be o.k. and not to worry, when he gets her home she can have a drink to calm her nerves.

So they pull up to Good's place and they both jump out and go inside quickly.

So they enter the spot and Good tells her that first things are first. She is going to have to dump her car because he probably knows her car and then she is going to have to change everything else too.

She is going to have to move out of her place because he knows where she lives.

He pours her a drink and then he lets her know that if his woman comes by and tries to get funky with her don't take it personal because she is just a jealous bitch and really don't mean no harm.

"I just been shot at and I aint got no time for no jealous bull shit Good" she tells him.

"I know but I'm just sayin because she has a key to get in and she could just pop up anytime" he tells her.

Frenchy is starting to calm down after taking a few more sips of drank and tells Good that she is ready for that bubble bath.

She has never been to Good's place so when she goes into the bathroom and sees the tub she gets really excited and can't help but to get loud.

"Danm Good, now that is a bathtub" she tells him.

"You can fit about four people in this tub" she adds on.

Good reaches into the sliding cupboard and pulls out some bubble bath and hands it to her.

"All I have is a t-shirt for you when you're done but it's better than nothing all, though I do like nothing better" he says.

She takes the bubble bath from him and tells him thanks.

"You are so good to me Goodnight. Thank you so very much" and looks him in the eyes.

"How can I ever repay you" she asks him as she starts taking off her clothes.

She takes off her top and then her pants standing there next to the tub, then she bends over pointing her ass right at Good and turns on the water.

Good loves they way she looks with her black panties on and her lace bra to match.

She makes sure that the water is just right and then she turns and looks Good right in the eyes and takes her bra off and then drops her panties.

Good stands there watching her for that moment and then he starts to take off his shirt. He tells her that he knows of a way she can repay him. Then he unfastens his pants and off they come.

Frenchy tells him to pass the bubble bath, so he does and then she pours some into the tub.

The bubbles are rising fast and she gets into the tub first and soon Good follows her. She kisses him once as they sit facing one another and then he kisses her back.

She scoots up closer to him and kisses him even more passionately and can't help but to notice his erection poking at her.

She grabs his hard penis and stokes it a couple of times as he touches and squeezes her tits.

Good tells her to stand up and bend over facing away from him so she does it. Then he tells her to back her ass up while still bending over.

He kisses her on the ass and she turns her head around to look at him.

He grabs a sponge and soaks it with water and then holds it over her ass and squeezes it as the warm wet water falls out on to her naked round ass.

He bits her ass and grabs her by the waist and pulls her closer to him.

He then starts biting her ass cheeks and licking her around her ass crack. She seems to love it as she turns her head straight forward and then back around to see what it is that he is doing that is driving her so mad.

He then starts to lick her ass cheeks from the top of her waist down to her vagina and then tells her to open wide.

"Open your legs wider" he tells her as he licks her fleshy vagina lips from behind.

"Back that ass up baby" he asks her as he licks in between her legs.

She is starting to moan now and tell him yes as she grinds backwards at his wanting mouth.

"You like that baby" he asks her.

"Oh, yes baby" she answers.

"I know just what you need baby" Good tells
her.

"Yes, I need you baby. I want you badly"
she tells him back.

Good then stands up so he can hit it from
behind doggy style but she tells him not so fast
and turns around and knees down in the water.
Then she starts to give him some head to show
her gratitude.

"Oh, yhea baby" he tells her.

"I know you like this" she answers back.

So after a couple more minutes go bye,
Good tell her to stand up and bend over. She
does and he slaps her on the ass and tells her
to spread her legs apart.

Frenchy spreads her legs and looks back at
Good as he stands out of the tub and pulls her
out of the tub also.

He grabs his hard erect penis and slowly slides it inside her soft and wet vagina. He eases only the head in and out as she licks her lips and moans for more.

"Yes Good" she says as she reaches around to touch his naked chest.

"You know what I like" Good tells her as he stokes her slowly and then speeds up but not to fast yet. He smacks her on the ass and she lets out an unexpected scream.

"Oh, yes" she says as he starts to stroke her a lil harder and lil faster. Then he shoves himself all the way inside of her and stops as she starts to shake and tell him that she loves it.

They continue to share passionate sex sounds back and forth and then all of a sudden Good stops and just looks at her.

"Whats wrong" Frenchy says.

"Nothing" he answers back.

"Why did you stop" she ask him.

"I'm really not feelin this right now" he says and starts to walk away from her.

Frenchy just looks at him and says "So your just going to leave me hear like this".

Good dosent even answer her back he just goes back into the bathroom and starts to turn on the water.

Frenchy gets up and walks over to the bathroom and looks inside the door and hits him on the arm.

"What's wrong" she ask him again. He looks at her and says "Your in love with Big and I cant do this to my homie". She looks down to the floor and starts to get sad understanding that Good is starting to really feel her and cares about her.

Frenchy walks over to the bed and falls down onto it. she rolls over and looks up to the ceiling and starts to think about Big. She wonders is she really in love with Big or is she just a user trying to get what she wants in life. She really needs his help to get rid of Dirt and she knows it. She also feels deeply about him and cares about him a lot.

Good comes out of the bathroom and tells her that he will be back in a little while. He walks over to the door and opens it, looks back and tells her not to wait up it might be awhile before he comes back because he has to take care of some things and also don't answer the phone.

She just watches him leave and a tear comes out of her eye.

Later she picks up the phone and calls Big.

"Hi Big, are you alright" she ask him.

"Hi baby, I'm fine" he replies.

"Are you o.k. babe" he asks her.

"Yes, I'm just shaken up a lil bit" she tells him.

"You'll be o.k. babe. Pour you a drink and calm your nerves" he tells her. She tells him to hold on as she goes to pour herself a drink. She comes back to the phone, sips her drink and tells Big I want that mother fucker dead. He almost killed me and everyone else in the club. Big agrees with her as she goes on...

"I'm so glad you were there for me baby" she tells Big.

"I love you so much" she says.

"I love you too baby" Big answers back.

"Don't worry about nothing babe, me and my boys are going to take care of this dude. Nobody comes to my town and does this to me or my boys" he tells her angrily.

"How's your arm baby" she asks him.

"It's o.k. my home girl Tish patched it up for me" he tells her.

"I gotta go babe, I got to finish what this punk started" he says.

"O.K. baby, please be careful" she tells him and they hang up their phones.

Big goes over to his boys house and they plan to take care of business with this Dirt.

So Dirt goes and gets some medical attention from one of his ex girlfriends and tells her all about what happened.

"It was crazy. It was like we walked into a trap or something" he tells her.

"They must have known that we were coming or something. It all happened so damn fast, it's like they were waiting for us or something" he just can't understand.

While his ex bandages his arm she tells him "You need to get the hell out of town as soon as possible".

So Dirt gets on the first thing out of Los Angeles and back to Louisiana he goes.

Chapter Twelve

As the days pass and things start to settle back down Dirt comes up with a plan. He decides to play it sneaky real dirty.

He plans to use Frenchy's mother to lure her back into his arms. He calls her girlfriend Lady and tells her to give him her new number or else.

So later Frenchy talks to Lady and she explains everything. Then she calls Dirt from a different phone and Dirt tells her if you love your mother you will meet me or something very bad will happen to her.

Frenchy knows that he means what he says about hurting her mother so she agrees to meet him but on her terms and she will call him back in a few days.

She thinks about what the hell is she going to do now and decides to call her good old friend Lady back.

She dials Lady's number and Lady answers the phone "Hello".

"Hi Lady" Frenchy asks.

"Frenchy" Lady replies sounding worried.

"Yhea, it's me" she answers back.

"Girl, what the hell are you going to do"? she asks her.

"You wont even guess all the shit I been into girl, we need to take care of this fool" she tells her.

"I need your help though" she adds.

"Anything babe, just tell me what's the problem" Lady tells her.

So Frenchy tells her about all the episodes' that lead up to her calling her and Lady just cant believe it.

"That no good as nigga threatened your mama girl" she says to Frenchy.

"Oh no. We can't have this shit". She tells her.

"You need to get rid of this fool for good babe" Lady tells her.

"I think I have a plan" Lady says in a sneaky way.

"I'll call you right back" she tells Frenchy and hangs up the phone.

Frenchy sits there and thinks about what kind of plan could Lady have. So after a few minutes the phone rings and its Lady.

"Hey Frenchy" Lady says.

"Yhea" Frenchy replies.

"I want you to say hi to my friend Diamond" she says to Frenchy.

"Hi Diamond" Frenchy says into the phone.

"Hello Frenchy" Diamond says back to her.

"You don't remember me but I think we have met before some time ago" she tells her.

"Really" Frenchy says sounding eager to know.

"Yhea we met years ago when you came by my shop and picked up some things and I let you have some purses and shoes" she tells her.

"I remember you" Frenchy sounds off loudly.

"You know that fool Dirt has done some really foul shit to me too girl, and almost had me killed and left me for dead" she tells her.

"Girl he's threatened to kill my mama"
Frenchy tells her.

"We gotta do something about this fool
Ladies" Lady joins into the conversation.

"What we gonna do" Frenchy asks.

Lady tells her I have a plan.
So as Lady explains the plan to the girls they all
agree that this is a dog ass nigga and he is
going to get what he deserves finally.

Later, Frenchy tells Good that she has a plan
to get Dirt and he goes crazy not believing that
she could be so stupid and that she is going to
get herself killed.

"He threatened my mama" she shouts at
him and he just stands there in disbelief.

She goes on and tells him that she is not
going to let him hurt her mother and she has no
choice but to meet him like he wants but she
does have a plan and not to worry about it.

"I got myself into this and I have to get
myself out of it" she tells him.

He looks at her and says nothing but nods
his head as to agree with her.

She tells him that she has to see Big and let him know also about what's about to happen, then she walks to the door and turns around to him and says "Don't worry, I have to do this" then she walks out of the door.

She gets into her new car and goes across town to see Big and let him know what is going on and tell him her plans to meet Dirt.

Big thinks that she is crazy and Dirt is going to kill her if she gives him a chance to.

She tells him also not to worry and everything is going to be alright. This is something that she has to do. He has threatened her mother and this is the only way to end this.

"I have to meet him or he will hurt or kill my mother" she tells Big.

"You're crazy, you can't do it" Big tells her.

"I have to. I got myself into this and I'm going to have to get myself out of this". She says.

He walks over to her and grabs her to hug her as if he might never see her again. She holds him tightly and softly tells him "Make love to me".

"Come on baby" he tells her as he starts to pull her toward the bed room.

Her mind races as she tries not to think about Good and Dirt. Big quickly pulls her into the room and starts kissing her. She puts her arms around him and pulls him against her wanting body.

"I'll do anything for you" Big tells her as he kisses her neck and blows softly into her ear.

"I know baby" she tells him "but I have to do this myself" she adds as she starts to pull off his shirt.

Big starts to unbuckle his pants and Frenchy starts to pull of her clothes also. Off comes her top and bra while his shirt and pants come off.

She takes off her pants and they both stand there half naked with only there underwear bottoms' on.

Frenchy steps over to Big slowly and reaches out to him. He reaches back and touches her hand, pulls her close him and kisses her passionately in the mouth.

He turns her to the bed and pushes her down on top of the bed. He stands there looking at her like she is about to be eaten. Then he reaches down and pulls off her panties slowly.

"Take off your underwear" she tells him.

He pulls off his boxers and throws them at her as he hangs with a semi hard on, then he climbs over her and kisses her more in the mouth. She starts breathing harder and pulls him closer then she grabs his ass cheeks.

As she reaches around front to his penis and stokes it slowly, it starts to get hard and erect.

"Baby you're so hard" she tells him.

"You do that to me babe" he answers back.

"I want you. Give it to me" she commands him.

Big slowly starts to go downward on her. As he moves from down the neck to her breast she moans and squirms. Then he kisses down to her stomach and then around navel. He licks her navel and then she pushes him down to her vagina.

He kisses her ever so gently around her vagina and then her thighs one at a time slowly, then licks up to her warm wet hole.

He licks around her opening first, moving to her clit, then he sucks her fleshy lips as this drives her crazy.

"That feels so good baby" she tells him.

"You like it baby" he asks her.

"Oh yes" she answers.

He then licks her opening and she loves it as she can't help but to make him very excited by sounding off in the heat of passion.

She moans, groans and can't help but to grind at his face slowly.

He then starts to probe her hole with his tongue in and out, a little faster at first and then even more faster. She tells him to give it to her as he is driving her crazy by purposely avoiding her clit.

Then he licks her clit really slow and gentle. He licks around it and then he licks it again. She starts to really squirm and grind his face. He knows that she is going to cum if he keeps it up and she tells him that she is probably going too.

"Cum for me baby" he tells her as he licks and concentrates on her clit.

"Yes baby" she answers back to him.

He starts to quickly tickle her clit by licking it really fast and gently. Then he sucks on it several times and she can't help but make him want her by telling him she is Cuming in such a inviting way.

She starts to shiver and tense up and he knows that she is Cuming so he slows up so she can really enjoy her orgasm.

"Oh baby, that was so good" she tells him. He slides up to her face and kisses her rite in the mouth.

"Give it to me" she orders him.

"Give it to me now" she demands.

He slides his hard erect penis inside her slowly and she takes it all proudly. She is so wet and warm and he loves it. He pushes himself slowly all the way inside of her.

"Yes baby, give it to me" she tells him.

Big starts to hump her slowly, long stroking her and putting his hands around her sexy waist. He can feel her throbbing inside as he pushes himself all the way inside her.

He starts to pump a little faster and harder as she sounds off with yes words and groans of delight.

"I'm going to cum again" she tells him.

"Cum on baby" he answers back while stroking her.

He pounds himself inside her and she starts to climax again.

"Yes baby" she screams several times as he pounds her warm wetness.

Just as she finishes Cumming all over his hardened penis, he tells her to turn over. So she turns over and points her ass right to him on all fours.

He slaps her on the ass cheek and grabs his hard slippery penis and slowly slides it inside her. She tells him again that she loves it as he stokes her from behind doggy style.

She grabs for the sheets as he stokes her and then she grabs for a pillow noticing that she is making a lot of noise. Big grabs her ass cheek and squeezes it as he strokes her from behind with no mercy.

Then he grabs both her ass cheeks with both hands and squeezes them both pulling them upward toward her back. She starts to scream out "Oh My Goodness".

He knows that she is really loving this because she starts to cum again almost immediately. He slows down his pace a little so she can enjoy her orgasm a little more.

"This is some good dick" she tells him.

Then he starts to slowly speed up the pace again. Pounding her slippery, wet, warm hole he starts to moan and she can feel him inside her throbbing.

After a few minutes of him pounding her she starts telling him "cum on baby".

"Ooh yhea" he answers.

"Cum on baby" she repeats over and over.

"Ooh yhea" he starts to repeat also.

"Yhea baby, I feel you" she tells him.

"I'm going to cum" he answers back to her stroking her harder.

"I'm Cumming baby, I'm Cumming" he shouts.

His body jerks and tenses up as he shoots cum inside of her. She begs for more and tells him to give it to her softly as he slows down the pace to a final halt.

Then he tries to pull out but stops and tells her to let him go because her pussy is so tight.

They both start to laugh and she says to him "you so crazy".

Big pulls out and kisses her on the ass cheek as she falls down to the bed on her stomach.

Big staggers over to the bathroom and turns on the hot water. Then he grabs a towel and wets it, rings it out and wipes himself off looking into the mirror at himself with a great big smile.

He finishes cleaning himself and brings Frenchy a warm wet towel. She grabs the towel and thanks him for it. He answers back your welcome baby.

"Are you O.K." he asks her as he stands there looking down at her.

"Yhea baby, I'm fine" she answers.
She lays there and starts to think about how much she loves Big and how she is going to get rid of Dirt.

Big climbs into bed next to her and they lay there and cuddle, and soon they both fall fast asleep.

Chapter Thirteen

Then next morning Frenchy wakes up and calls her friend Lady in New Orleans.

"Hey girl" Lady answers the phone.

"Hey now" Frenchy says back to her.

"So what's up" Lady asks her.

"I think I'm ready to do this" she tells her.

"Are you sure" Lady asks her.

"Yhea, I'm sure" she replies.

"O.K. Hold on" she tells her as she puts her on hold and calls up someone on the conference line.

"You there" she asks Frenchy as she clicks her back on.

"Yhea I'm here" she answers.

The phone rings and a male someone answers the phone.

"Good morning, FBI. Green speaking. How can I help you" he says.

"Hi Detective Green, this is Lady. I called you last night and spoke with you" she says to him.

"Oh yes I remember. How are you" he asks her.

"I'm fine, thank you. I have my friend that I was telling you about on the line" she tells him.

"Say Hi Frenchy" she tells Frenchy.

"Hello Mr. Green" she says nervously.

"Hello Frenchy" he says back to her.

"I understand that you ladies have a problem with a known gang banger" he says.

"Yhea, He has threatened her mother Detective Green" Lady tells him.

"He's also a drug dealer and he tried to kill me" Frenchy adds in.

"O.K. so has any of you ladies talked to the police or anyone else about this" the detective asks them.

"No" both of the ladies reply at the same time.

"O.K. so I have a plan since me and Lady have known each other for a long time, I will help you ladies out" he says.

He tells Lady the he will meet her and explain all about it, he doesn't want to talk about it on his job phone. She agrees and they both tell Frenchy that everything is going to be all right and not to worry.

Frenchy agrees and tells Lady that she will talk to her after they get together and talk about the plan. They all say goodbye and hang up their phones.

Frenchy goes into the room where Big is still sleeping and wakes him up with a kiss.

"Good morning babe" Big tells her.

"Good morning honey" she answers.

"Are you hungry" she asks him.

"I sure am baby" he answers back.

"Well I can cook up some sausage and eggs if you like" she tells him.

"That sounds great baby" he says as he smiles at her.

So she starts to walk out of the bedroom and says it will be ready in fifteen minutes as she goes into the kitchen.

She whips up a quick breakfast for them and Big gets up and they both dig in and clean both of their plates.

"That was good baby. You sure can cook" he tells her as he winks his eye at her.

"Thanks baby. I'm glad you liked it" she tells him as she clears the table off. She walks over to the sink with the plates and puts them into the sink.

"You know I was thinking and I'm going to get that fool Dirt" she tells Big. Big looks at her as his eye brows go up and he says "Baby you should let me take of this shit. You might get yourself hurt of worse" he tells her.

"Your right" she says as she knows that Big is not going to go for her getting involved with that fool Dirt.

"Don't worry baby, I'll take care of that fool" he says as he stands up from the table.

"I'm going to go see my boys right now" he tells her as he goes into the room to get dressed.

Frenchy starts to wash the dishes and thinks about what might the detective and Lady be planning. All kinds of shit is going threw her head.

So after she cleans the kitchen up she tells Big that she is going out to get some air and that she has to clear her mind.

Meanwhile back in New Orleans the detective and Lady meet and talk about what they are going to do about Dirt.

So he tells her all about what to do to get rid of him for good and she agrees with it. They both leave and she calls up Frenchy and tells her the plan.

"Don't be scared girl, I think this shit might work and you won't have to worry about this fool never again" Lady tells Frenchy.

"O.K. but I sure hope that it works" she tells Lady in a nervous sounding voice.

"Don't worry baby, it will work" she answers.

They detective gets back to his office and pulls up some info on Dirt. He sees that he has had a ruff life as a teenager and quite a few run-in's with the police.

He pulls up some flight info him and sees that he was definitely in L.A. last month. He calls up Lady and asks if they can try to prove that Dirt was in the club that day they told him about. She says that maybe they can see if the club had some security cameras around the place.

Lady calls up Frenchy and asks her if the club had any security cameras to prove that Dirt was there or saw him do anything. She tells her that she can check and see.

So Frenchy goes and gets into her car and calls up Good. He answers the phone in a surprised mood. They talk for awhile and then he agrees to meet her at the club. She drives over to the club to see Good and he meets her out in the parking lot. As she pulls up he is already there and waiting for her.

She puts her window down as she rolls up to him and says "Hey babe, how you doin"?

He smiles back at her and says "Hey good looking". She parks her car and he meets her as she gets out of her car and gives her a great big hug and kiss.

"You know I been thinking about you" he tells her as he slides his hands down her waist touching her ass.

"I been thinking about so much shit lately I can't lie. I haven't really had time to think about anybody" she tells him.

"Well I know what you mean. Come on lets go inside" he tells her as he grabs her hand and they walk inside the club.

They go into the back room and Goodnight tells her "I got just what you need".

He pulls up the video surveillance tape of when Dirt came to the club and they watch it for awhile and Good stops it right at a spot where Dirt's face is right in front of the camera.

"Yes" Frenchy screams out loud.

"I got you now" she adds.

So Good burns her a copy of the video and gives it to her. She is so happy and gives Good a great big hug and kiss. He looks at her and wonders what the hell is she up to but holds his tongue on asking her.

"Thank you so much" she tells him.

"Your welcome baby" he tells her.

"You know in a strange way, I do love you" Good says to her.

"She looks back at him and says "I love you too".

So as Frenchy leaves, she gets into her car and calls up Lady.

"Hey Lady, I got some surveillance of Dirt's ass right in front of the camera girl" she says in a cheerful way.

"O.K. can you email it to me" Lady asks her.

"Sure thing, just let me get home and I'll upload it to my computer" she tells her.

"O.K. I'll be waiting for it. Let me know when you do it" Lady tells her.

"Oh" Lady adds.

"I talked to Diamond and she said that she is so down to help us" she says excitedly.

"Great" Frenchy says.

"I'll call you when I get home" she tells her before she hangs up. They both hang up and Frenchy continues on driving to get home.

So Frenchy pulls up at home, walks in and uploads the video on her computer. Then she sends the email to Lady.

She picks up her phone and calls Lady up. The phone rings.

"Hello" Lady answers.

"Hey girl, I sent you the video" she tells her.

"O.K. cool. I'll forward it to the detective" she answers back to Frenchy.

"So let me know what happens with it" she says to Lady.

"Oh you know I will. You know this" she tells her giggling.

"Let me do this and I'll get right back at you" Lady tells her and then they both hang up the phone.

So Lady emails the detective Green and then calls him up on the phone.

"Hello Lady" he asks.

"Hello detective Green. It's me" she answers.

"I sent you a email of video with him at the club" she adds.

"Oh, great" he tells her.

"I'll check it out and call you back in about an hour" he tells her.

She agrees and then they both hang up. So while the detective looks at the video, the girls get a conference call going between Lady, Frenchy and Diamond.

They discus and talk about how they can lure Dirt into a trap and then trap him for good.

After about 45 minutes of going back and forth about it, they come up with a brilliant plan.

So they hang up and then Lady calls up Dirt and tells him that she knows Frenchy and that she is interested in meeting and she wants to make up because she still loves him.

Dirt is skeptical about it but he does still have feelings for Frenchy. So he agrees to meet with her in Los Angeles. He tells Lady to have her call him. She agrees and they hang up.

Lady calls up Frenchy and tells her that Dirt wants to talk to her and she tells Lady that she must be crazy but she will call him and she excepted the phone number.

So Frenchy thinks about it for awhile and then gets up enough nerve to call Dirt. She dials the number slowly and then finally she hears the phone ringing.

"Hello" Dirt answers.

"Hi Dirt" Frenchy says.

"Frenchy" he asks sounding surprised and happy.

"Yhea, it's me" she answers.

"Your voice still sounds the same" he tells her.

"I'm so sorry she tells him" sounding as if she was going to cry.

"I didn't really want to hurt you but I was just so mad at them fools for taking you from me" he tells her.

"Do you forgive me" she asks him.

"I love you" she adds.

"I forgive you and I love you too" he tells her.

"I have to tell you something, tell me you won't get mad at me" she asks.

"Go ahead, tell me but I caint promise that I won't get mad" he tells her.

"I have been with a woman also" she says to him and there is a brief moment of silence.

"That's cool. I can live with that" he tells her.

"I've been with a woman and a man at the same time" she adds.

"Oh really" he says back to her.

"Yhea, it kinda just happened and I enjoyed it" she tells him.

"So you roll like that huh" he asks her.

"Not really, it was just that one time" she tells him.

"So did you do her or did she do you" he asks her.

"We both did each other and him as well" she tells him.

"Damn girl I'm getting excited just thinking about that" he tells her.

"I know it's making my panties wet just thinking about it too" she adds.

"Hey do you remember the girl a long time ago named Diamond. I took you over there and she gave you some stuff" he asks her.

"Yhea, I remember her, she grabbed my ass when I was leaving and I think that's what started it all. I really didn't mind" she tells him.

"No shit" he says.

"Well maybe you can bring her out with you and we can get together the three of us" she suggests to him.

"You know that's a good idea" he says.

"I'll talk to her and see if she is down" he adds.

"I cant wait to see you" she tells him.

"I cant wait to see you too baby" he tells
her.

"So I'll talk to you soon, o.k." she tells him
as she rushes him off the phone.

"O.K. so I got to go right now. I'm at work
and I'll call you later" she tells him just to get
him off the phone.

"All right, I'll talk to you later" Dirt tells her
and then they both hang up the phones.

Frenchy almost immediately goes' into the
bathroom and looks into the mirror at herself.

She turns on the water and splashes some
on her face, then she dry's her face back off.
She looks into the mirror once more and tells
herself I've got to do this.

So she goes back into the front room and
picks up the phone to call Lady. She punches in
her number, the phone rings and Lady picks up.

"Hello" Lady says.

"Hi Lady" Frenchy answers.

"What's up" she asks her.

"I just talked to Dirt and he agreed to meet
me" she tells her.

"Are you serious" she shouts into the phone.

"Yhea girl, he said he would come out to L.A. to meet me" she tells her.

"I told him that you still loved him and he fell for it" Lady says.

"I just hope this works and we get rid of this fool for good" Frenchy says.

"As long as you stay cool and focused, it will work" she tells her.

They go on back and forth for a while and then they hang up.

So later that day the detective calls up Frenchy and talks to her about how they could set this Dirt bag up. She listens and they both agree to how the detective is trying to set him up. He finishes explaining all of the details and Frenchy agrees again to his plan. They hang up their conversation and Frenchy thinks it all over in her head.

Frenchy calls up Lady to fill her in on all the details of how this is going to work. She tells Lady that the plan is to tell Dirt that she has some money for him as well as her love, so he doesn't try to kill her before he gets the money.

She knows that he is money hungry and he will take the bait if money is involved.

So time passes on and she finally gets to the day that Dirt is coming to L.A. and she is very nervous.

Dirt calls her from New Orleans and lets her know what time the plane will land and to meet him there. He also lets her know that Diamond is going to be with him.

So Frenchy gets to the airport before they land, parks the car and just sits there for a minute to gather her nervous self.

The plane lands and Dirt and Diamond get off the plane and start walking down the terminal to get to the baggage department to get their bags.

Dirt calls up Frenchy on the phone to let her know their on their way. She answers the phone.

"Hello" she says.

"Hey baby, were here" he tells her.

"O.K. What baggage claim area are you guys in" she ask him.

"I don't know they haven't told us yet" he says.

"I will just meet you down there" she tells him and he agrees and they both hang up their phones.

Frenchy walks into the bag area and looks for Dirt and Diamond but doesn't see them. She walks over to the TV monitors to see what claim area they will be at and as she is looking up at the monitors she feels someone from behind grab her ass. She turns around quickly and looks to see Diamond smiling at her.

"Hey girl" Diamond tells her.

"Hey" she answers back.

"Dirt went to the bathroom, he'll be right out" she says.

"Oh, o.k." Frenchy says.

"Girl you look a little nervous, what's wrong" she asks her.

"Oh, nothing. I'm all right" she answers back to Diamond.

"You sure" Diamond asks her.

"Well you know he did try to kill me the last time I saw him" she tells her and Diamonds eyes got really big.

"You didn't know that" Frenchy asks her.

"No, I didn't" she answers back.

Then she sees Dirt come from around the corner and he recognizes Frenchy and his eyes light up and he puts on a great big smile. As he walks up to Frenchy she puts her arms out to give him a big hug. He hugs her back and gives her a big kiss and so she kisses him back.

"Don't mind me" Diamond says while she stands there and watches them hug and kiss.

"I'm sorry, you already know Diamond right" he asks Frenchy.

"Yes" she answers and they all walk over to the carousel to find there bags. They talk a little but Dirt does not let her hand go. He holds on to her hand as if he does not want to loose her again.

"There's my bag" Diamond says as she reaches for it.

"And here comes yours" she tells Dirt. Dirt reaches for his bag and finally lets go of Frenchy's hand.

He pulls his bag off the carousel and asks Frenchy were did she park and she answers across the street.

She starts to walk out of the terminal and looks back to see if they are following her and they are.

She waits for Dirt and holds his arm just to make him feel good.

"We have to cross here" she tells them as the walk light turns green.

They all walk across the street into the parking structure and she shows them were the car is. She pushes the alarm button and you hear the car chirp. Diamond says to her "You got a really nice car girl".

"Thanks girl" she answers back.

"You rollin like this" Dirt asks her.

"You like it baby" she asks him.

"Hell Yhea" he answers back.

She pops the trunk and Dirt puts all the bags inside. He closes the trunk and they get inside the car and close the doors.

Frenchy starts up the car and backs out of the parking spot. She puts it in drive and they start on there way.

"I know a really nice hotel you guys can stay at and they got some good ass lobster too" Frenchy tells them.

"How was the flight" she asks them just to keep the conversation going.

"It was cool" Dirt tells her.

"Yhea it was all right" Diamond adds.

They keep on there way and soon they pull up at the hotel. Frenchy stops at the front door and the bell man walks up to the car and ask them if they need any help.

"Yhea man you can get the bags out of the trunk" Dirt tells him.

Frenchy and Diamond look at each other as they both knew he had no class at all. So the bell man gets their bags out of the trunk and takes them to the counter to check in.

At the counter the agent asks for some Identification and Frenchy says that she left hers at home and Dirt pulls his out and says we can put it in his name.

They fill out the paperwork and the agent gives them two keys and tells the bell hop what room their in.

"This way please" the bell hop tells them as he walks toward the elevators. They follow him.

The elevator rings and the doors open up. The bell man goes in first and holds the doors open as they follow him inside. He presses the tenth floor button and the doors close them all inside.

They reach the tenth floor and everyone exits the elevator and walks down to the room. The bell man opens their room and everyone goes inside and he puts their luggage into the closet area then pulls his cart out of the room and stands at the door and asks them "Is that all sir" as he folds his arms with his hand open facing the ceiling as if he was waiting for a tip.

Dirt just looks at him and then Frenchy says "Yes that will be all, thank you" as she hands him a ten dollar bill.

"Thank you so very much" he tells her as he turns around and walks away.

She closes the door behind him and almost immediately Dirt asks her "So where's the money".

She looks at him and says "it's in the bank".

"I'll get it in the morning" she tells him.

"I had to order the cash in advance" she adds.

"Well I brought my own money" Diamond says.

"You know I'm ready to do some shopping" she adds with a big smile on her face.

"Can we get a car like you said" Diamond asks Dirt.

"Yhea" he answers.

"Can you take us to go get a rental car" he asks Frenchy.

"Sure I can" she tells him.

"Let's go right now and get it over with" Diamond says as she walks over to the door.

"I have to meet with some clients later on so I'll come back tonight and spend more time with you guys" Frenchy tells them.

"That's cool" Diamond says

"I hope it doesn't take to long I didn't come all the way out here not to see you" Dirt tells Frenchy

"Don't worry babe, It wont take to long I just have to get some papers signed and that's it" she tells him.

So they walk out of the door and go down stairs to the car. They get inside the car and head down to the car rental place. Dirt uses his license to rent the car also and they get a really nice one too.

So Frenchy tells them that she will be back in a few hours and they say there good-byes as she gets in her car and leaves then Dirt and Diamond go back to the hotel.

Frenchy gets to house and she calls up Lady and tells her that they bought it and everything is going as planned.

Lady tells her that she will be right over. Lady gets in her car and leaves her hotel and starts to Frenchy's place. She had to come all the way out here just for this and wouldn't miss it for the world.

So Lady gets to Frenchy's and they sit at the table and open a bag that Lady had brought over.

"This is what they call C4" she tells Frenchy.

"It looks like play dough" she tells Lady.

"This aint nothing to play with baby. This will blow some shit up for real" she tells Frenchy.

Frenchy then gets a bag that she had under her bed, puts it on the table and opens it.

"Now this is some real shit too" she tells Lady.

"Pure cocaine" she adds.

"Half a kilo" she tells Lady.

So they put both the small bags into a bigger bag and then they say "I think were ready".

"Wait" Frenchy says.

She goes into the bedroom and gets a brown paper bag from under the bed with something in it. She unfolds the bag and pulls out a 9mm hand gun but just enough so Lady can see it without her touching it. She puts it back into the bag and folds it up.

Frenchy puts the gun into the bag with the dope and the explosives then looks at Lady.

"I think were ready now" she says as she smiles.

"I think were ready" Lady agrees.

So Frenchy calls up Dirt and asks him if Diamond had left shopping and he tells her "Yhea she's gone".

"Are you on your way" he asks her.

"Yhea in a few minutes, I'll be on my way" she tells him.

"O.K. I'll see you soon" he tells her and hangs up because he has no patience.

So Frenchy calls up Diamond and tells her that they are ready and she can meet them now.

Diamond says o.k. and tells them were she is and to meet her there at that location.

So about ten minutes pass and Frenchy and Lady pull up to the parking lot where Diamond is waiting. They see her and pull up next to her and park.

"Hey girl" Lady says to her.

"Hey girl" Diamond says back to Lady.

"Hey girl" Frenchy says to Diamond also.

Then Diamond opens up the trunk and they put the bag with the gun, dope and explosives inside of her trunk and then close it.

They look at each other and say "This is going to work right" and they all agree.

So Diamond goes back to the room and Lady and Frenchy go back home for a short minute.

Frenchy calls up Dirt and tells him that she is on her way, she will be right there.

"It's about time" he tells her and then Diamond says that she is hungry and she wants to get something to eat.

"We will get something when my baby gets here" Dirt tells Diamond.

"O.K." she agrees with him.

"I'm hungry too" he adds.

Soon Frenchy knocks on the door and Dirt answers the door and tells her "It's about time. Damn, what took you so long" He asks her.

"I didn't think I took that long baby" she tells him.

"We are starving girl" Diamond tells her.

"So what do you want to eat" Frenchy asks her.

"What's up with that lobster you was talking about" she says. Dirt just goes along with it and says "Yhea, what's up with the lobster".

"It's right down stairs" Frenchy tells them.

"It's a twenty minute wait" she adds.

"Damn, it better be good, a nigga gotta wait all that time" Dirt tells her.

"It's worth the wait baby come on lets go" Frenchy tells him.

"You guys go ahead and order me one too. I have to use the bathroom and take a shower first" Diamond tells them.

"All right, but you better hurry up. If you aint there in twenty minutes I'm gone eat yours too" Dirt tells Diamond.

Chapter Fourteen

So Frenchy and Dirt leave and get into the elevator to go eat. Diamond stays behind and waits for Frenchy to call her.

Dirt and Frenchy gets their sets in the restaurant and Frenchy says to Dirt "I'm going to wash my hands I'll be right back".

She gets up and goes into the bathroom and calls Diamond and tells her that they are sitting at the table and going to order.

"Starting operation shut down" Diamond tells Frenchy.

They hang up the phones and Frenchy goes back out to the table and sits there with Dirt.

As they wait for a waiter to take their order down stairs, Diamond is at work upstairs.

Diamond stands in front of a mirror looking at herself then all of a sudden she smashes her head into the mirror and it cuts her face.

Then she walks out of the bathroom and runs into the picture hanging on the wall and breaks it and cuts her arm.

Then she throws herself on top, against the dresser and smashes that mirror too. She starts to punch herself in the face and nose and her nose starts to bleed then she turns over one of the night stands and it breaks also.

Then she picks up the phone, calls 911 and tells them that her pimp has kicked her ass and has threatened to kill her, please come right away.

So meanwhile downstairs, they are sitting at the table waiting for the lobster tails and hear some police siren's getting closer and closer.

Then they see a police car stop in front of the hotel and some police run inside and then another police car pulls up and then the ambulance runs inside and they think nothing of it.

So after a few minutes a police officer comes into the restaurant and stops at the door. He looks at Dirt and immediately gets on the radio as if he was calling for backup.

Another cop comes into the restaurant and then another. Dirt notices that they are all looking at him and is getting nervous but doesn't know why.

Two cops walk over to the table with their hands on there guns and tell Dirt "Sir we need you to come outside".

"For what" he answers back.

"Sir we need you to come outside right now" the officer tells him.

Dirt stands up and starts to walk outside and one of the cops grab him and puts his hands behind his back. Then he quickly puts the cuffs on him.

"What the hell is going on" Dirt shouts out loud.

"Baby no" Frenchy says out loud.

The cops take him outside and throw him on the hood of one of the cop cars. They pat him down and then put him in the back of one of the police cars.

As he looks out of the window he can see the paramedic walking out with Diamond and she looks like she just got the shit kicked out of her.

She gets closer to the police car and starts screaming "That's that mother fucker right there".

"I hope they kick your ass mother fucker" she adds and then tells the cops to look in his car trunk.

"He's got guns and drugs in his trunk" she tells the cops.

Dirt is looking at all this in amazement wondering what the hell is going on.

Two cops go around to the rental car and open the trunk and find a bag with half a kilo of cocaine, some C4 explosives and a 9mm Glock.

They bring all this stuff out and around to the sergeant on the scene and he just shakes his head. He walks over to the car that Dirt is in and ask him "So what are you doing with all this stuff".

Dirt just looks at him shocked and still trying to figure out what the hell has just happened.

The Sergeant starts to read him his rights.

"You have the right to remain silent" he tells him.

"Anything you say can be used against you in a court of law".

"You have the right to an attorney, while you are being questioned".

"If you can't afford an attorney, the court will appoint one to you free of charge".

"Do you understand these rights" the cop finishes telling him.

He just shakes his head in shock as Frenchy stands their looking at him as if she doesn't know what the hell is going on but has a smirk on her face also.

A cop comes over to Frenchy and asks if she is all right and she says yes. The cop goes on to tell her that this guy is a piece of shit and is a pimp that beat up one of his hoes.

"They found all kinds of drugs and guns in his car and some explosives too" the cop goes on to tell her.

"He may actually be given a terrorist sentence for the explosives" another cop walks up and tells Frenchy.

"He is looking at a lot of time, that's for sure" he adds on.

Frenchy gets on the phone and calls up Lady to tell her what has happened to Dirt.

"Hello" Lady answers the phone.

"Hi Lady" Frenchy greets her.

"What's going on" Lady inquires.

"Well the found everything in the trunk and now have him in the back of a police car and one of the cops said that he is going to get a lot of time for all the stuff they found" she says.

"Sounds like it worked" Lady tells her.

"Yes, I sure hope so" Frenchy says back to her.

"So how is Diamond" Lady asks.

"She looked fucked up, but I think she will be all right" she answers.

"I'm going to the hospital to see her now" Frenchy adds.

"I'll meet you there. Which one is she at" she asks.

"I think there taking her to Kaiser on Cadillac Street by the ten freeway" she tells her.

"I'll meet you there" she tells her and they both say goodbye and hang up the phones.

So Frenchy goes over to the sergeant and asks him if they are going to take the girl to Kaiser on Cadillac Street and he confirms that they are. So she goes and gets into her car and starts to drive over to the hospital to see Diamond.

Meanwhile Lady calls up detective Green and tells him that the plan worked and they have Dirt in custody.

"I will send them the video of him at the club and tell them that this is the guy behind the shoot out and the deaths at the club" the detective tells Lady.

"O.K. and thank you so very much for helping us out" Lady tells the detective.

"Your very welcome Lady" he answers.

"What are friends for" he adds.

"So I'll see you later and we have to do lunch" she tells him.

"All right, I'll talk to you later" he says.

They both say goodbye and hang up their phones.

So the detective calls up the Los Angeles Police Department and tells them all about the video and sends it right over to them. They look at the video and conclude that this is the same guy and add several more charges to his list of crimes. So Dirt will definitely be going away for a very long long time.

Frenchy gets to the hospital and waits for Lady to get there before she goes inside to see Diamond.

As she waits for Lady a dirty beggar walks up to her and asks her if she has any spare change. She tells him no and he starts to walk away then she stops him and tells him to come back.

"I think I might have some change" she tells him.

She reaches into her pocket book and pulls out a twenty dollar bill and then hands it to the bum.

"Here you are" she tells him as she puts the twenty dollar bill in his hand. He looks at her and smiles brightly at her.

"Thank you so much" he tells her as he bows his head several times and walks backward out of the waiting area.

Seconds later a security guard walks inside and asks if anyone has seen a bum come inside here. No one answers him and Diamond just smiles and laughs.

Lady walks in minutes later and Frenchy gets up and gives her a great big hug.

"We did it" she tells Frenchy.

"The detective Green is sending the cops the video of Dirt at the club and he is going away for a very long time" she adds.

"I'm so glad it's over" Frenchy tells Lady.

"You mama is safe now" Lady says to Frenchy.

"We owe it all to Diamond" Frenchy tells her.

"Let's go see her" Lady says and they both start to walk into the emergency room. They asks a nurse about a victim that came in recently and she says that she is right over there. They walk over to the room where she is laying on a bed and walk inside.

"Hi Diamond" they both say at the same time almost.

"Hey girls" Diamond answers back.

"Are you o.k." Frenchy asks her.

"Yhea I'm fine" she says back.

"You don't look fine" Lady tells her.

"I'm o.k." she answers back.

"So Dirt is going away for a very long time" Lady tells Diamond.

"It's all thanks to you Diamond" Frenchy tells her.

"Thank you so very much" she adds.

"Your welcome" Diamond tells Frenchy.

"I owe you big time girl" Frenchy tells her.

"Don't worry about it" she answers.

A Doctor walks in the room and tells Diamond that she is going to be alright and that she only has a couple of scratches to live with. She can leave in a few minutes. Diamond thanks the doctor and he walks back out of the room.

"So we will get you out of here and you can stay with me for the time being" Frenchy tells Diamond.

"Are you sure" she answers.

"Girl that's the least that I can do for you" she tells her.

"Well I'm starving" Frenchy says.

"Me too" Lady adds.

"Me three" Diamond agrees.

Then a nurse walks into the room and hands Diamond a release form to sign. She signs it and the nurse tells her that she can get dresses now.

"Well I got some clothes for you at my place" Frenchy tells Diamond.

"So I will meet you girls at Frenchy's place" Lady says and they all agree. Diamond gets dressed in the bloody clothes and they all leave the hospital and head over to Frenchy's place.

They get over to Frenchy's and find something for Diamond to wear in her closet. Then they all go out to eat.

The dinner is great and they all are laughing and having a ball together drinking a few drinks and celebrating there big achievement.

"Thanks for everything Diamond" Frenchy tells her.

"Oh, your welcome Frenchy" she answers.

"I really owe you a lot" Frenchy adds.

"Well ok if you say so" she answers and they all start laughing.

"No, seriously. I want to give you something" she says.

"Lets get out of here and I have something at home I want to give you" she tells Diamond with a smile on her face.

"All right" she says and smiles back at Frenchy.

They flag down the waiter and asks for the check. The waiter brings them over their bill and Frenchy says "this one is one me ladies" and pulls out some cash then pays for their dinner and drinks.

They all get up and walk outside to there cars and Lady says "I will catch up to you ladies later; I have an old friend to see out here".

"All right, so we will see you later" Frenchy tells Lady and they get into there cars and head out their separate ways.

Meanwhile Dirt is getting booked into jail and still can't really figure out where it all went wrong.

"Hey inmate" a cop shouts at Dirt.

"You got any health problems" the cop asks.

"No" he answers as he shakes his head.

"Strip down" the cop shouts at him again in a commanding voice. So Dirt starts to take his clothes off and strips down to nothing and the cop tells him to turn around and spread his ass cheeks. So he does.

"Cough" the cop tells him and he does it.

"Lift your feet up one at a time" he orders him and he does it.

"Now lift your ball sack" he tells him and Dirt grabs his ball sack and lifts it up.

The cop gives him his new jail clothes and some linen then tells him and a few others to go into the next room.

So they go into the next room and sit there and wait for an hour and then all of the sudden a fight breaks out and two guys beat the shit out of one poor dude for staring at one of the guys tattoos.

They both punch and kick on him till he hits the floor and curls up. Then one of the guys starts kicking him in the stomach and the face and everyone just watches and no one says anything.

After they stop fighting or should I say kicking his ass, the guy just lies there for a moment and then he gets up and sits there in the corner and doesn't say a word.

Dirt looks at one of the guys' tattoo that was in the fight and quickly looks away. The tattoo says SOUTHSIDE in big bold letters across his lower stomach.

"So anybody else got a problem with my tattoo" the guy says out loud as he holds his arms out to the side. No one says a word and everyone looks scared that they might be next.

"Southside don't take no shit" the guy shouts out loud.

Dirt starts realizing that he is a long way from the Dirty South and that is what he has tattooed on his stomach. He starts to think that it's only a matter of time before someone sees it and then he notices that one of the guys in the strip down is looking at him.

He is starring at him and has a very serious look on his face. Dirt is no punk, so he stairs back at him but doesn't say anything. The guy starts to mean mug him with a mad dog face and then says to him "What the fuck you looking at".

"What you looking at" Dirt answers back to him and tension fills the room quickly.

"I'm lookin at a bitch ass fool from the dirty south" the guy tells Dirt.

"I saw your tattoo on your stomach" the guy tells Dirt.

"So what" Dirt answers back nervously.

"This is L.A. fool and we don't like the south" the guy tells him and stands up.

Dirt stands up and the other two guys that were in the fight stand up also. At that moment Dirt knows he is going to get his ass kicked but he aint going out without a fight.

"I aint no easy win" Dirt tells them as they start to walk over towards him. Then all the sudden a cop comes up and says "let's go inmates, time to move it out".

They look at Dirt and one of the guys wink at him while the other tells him "We got your number fool".

The cop opens the cage and tells them to stay on the yellow line against the wall.

"If anyone gets out of line they will get there ass kicked" the cop shouts at them.

So they all leave the holding cell and start to follow the yellow line into the next holding cell area where they are being separated according to danger level.

Murderers are separated form petty crimes and the gang members are separated from each other so they don't kill one another.

Dirt is put in a cell with some guy that has been already locked up for several years and has already adjusted to the system.

The cop locks down the cell and walks off.

"So what you in for celly" the guy asks Dirt.

"These bitches set me up with some explosives, guns, dope and money" he tells the guy.

"So they got you for criminal use of explosives, drug trafficking, a concealed weapon and drug money" the guy answers back to him.

Dirt just looks at him and the guy says to him "You're fucked".

"Are you on probation or parole" he asks Dirt.

"I'm on parole" Dirt answers as he shakes his head.

"Well my man, looks like there going to throw the book at you and you might get life or even worse" he says to Dirt.

Dirt just looks at him in disbelief as he still can't understand how this all happened so fast. He thought his game was so tight and thought out.

Chapter Fifteen

Meanwhile Frenchy and Diamond get back to her place and they go inside. Frenchy tells her to have a seat, so she does while Frenchy goes into the bedroom and goes over to her safe.

She punches in the combination and opens up the safe door. Then she grabs twenty thousand dollars and closes the safe back. She walks into the front room and hands Diamond the money.

"What's this" Diamond asks her.

"That's yours" she tells her.

"It's only a token for your help" Frenchy adds.

"I don't know what to say" Diamond tells her.

"Don't say anything" she tells her and bends down and kisses her in the lips.

Diamond drops the money and is in shock. Frenchy asks her if she likes that and she agrees that she does.

Frenchy grabs her hand and guides her up into the bedroom. She sits her on the bed and stands there in front of her looking her in the eyes.

Frenchy starts to take her clothes off slowly and starts to give Diamond a smile. Off comes her shirt and then she takes off her bra.

Diamond stares at her breast and Frenchy steps closer to her as if she wants her to kiss them.

Diamond leans foward to kiss her breast. She touches one of them and eases her fingers up to her nipple. She squeezes the nipple and then she leans over and kisses it.

Frenchy grabs the back of her head and Diamond starts to suck her tit, licking and squeezing it.

Then she changes to the other side and Frenchy is enjoying it because she is making some yes sounds and tells her "that feels good".

Diamond's hands start to slowly slide down her side to her hips and then around to her pants buttons. She starts to unbutton her pants and Frenchy tells her "Let me help you" as she unfastens her pants and tells her to take off her clothes.

Diamond stands up and starts to undress and before you could say ass bucked naked they were both ass naked.

Frenchy pushes Diamond down onto the bed, climbs over her and starts kissing her tits. She slowly caresses her breast and then moves her hand down her stomach to her vagina. She softly touches her around her opening and then she slides her fingers around the outside of her clit.

"Oh, that feels good" Diamond tells her.

"Ssshhh, don't say a word" Frenchy tells her as she gently caresses her soft wetness.

Frenchy notices that she is starting to feel how hot, wet and slippery she is getting so she slides the tip of her finger just inside her.

Diamond squirms and moans as if she is really enjoying this.

Frenchy uses the wetness of her vagina to play around her clit but being very careful not to touch it yet.

She moves her finger back down and gets some more of her slippery wetness and then back up to her clit she goes.

First she plays around her clit and then she touches it oh so very gently. This is driving Diamond crazy and she knows it because she is moaning and groaning and squirming like a fish out of water.

Frenchy stops her foreplay and moves in for the kill by kissing her stomach and moving down to her soft and wet garden.

She licks around her vagina lips up and down and around and then she tickles her opening with the tip of her tongue. Diamond is so wet and excited that she starts to cum.

"I'm going to cum" she tells Frenchy.

Then Frenchy starts to lick her clit and Diamond start to quiver. She licks around her clit and then sucks it so very gently and more licking and more sucking.

"I'm Cuming, I'm Cuming" Diamond shouts as she grabs the back of Frenchy's head.

Frenchy starts to slow down and just licks around her clit and lets Diamond cum with pleasure.

"Oh my goodness, that was so good" Diamond tells her.

"I'm glad you liked it, you're my first" Frenchy tells her.

"Your first what" Diamond asks her.

"I never been with a female before" she tells her.

"Now I really feel special" Diamond answers her back.

Diamond sits up on the bed and tells Frenchy to lie down on the bed. Frenchy lays back on the bed and Diamond climbs over the top of her and looks her in the eyes.

Diamond kisses Frenchy on the forehead and kisses each eye lid slowly. Then she rubs noses with her and kisses her in the lips long and slow. Frenchy grabs her ass and pulls her toward her closer.

"You want me don't you" Diamond asks her.

"Yes" she answers and hesitates.

"Yes I do" she says again as Diamond kisses her on the neck. Then she moves down and kisses her on each breast tickling her nipples' with the tip of her tongue.

"I know what you like" Diamond tells her.

She looks Frenchy in the eyes and Frenchy stairs back at her.

"Yes, you do" Frenchy tells her as she guides her head down between her legs. Diamond starts to kiss her wet vagina and they moan together to let each other know that they are enjoying each others company.

"Do you like that" Diamond asks Frenchy as she licks her vagina lips and sucks her clit.

"Mmmmm hmmmm" Frenchy answers.

Diamond starts to lick around her clit and suck it gently. She tells her to cum for her as she sucks and licks around her clit faster and more aggressively.

"Oohh, that feels so good" she tells Diamond.

"Your gonna make me cum" Frenchy says as she starts to grind her face.

"Cum for me boo" Diamond tells her.

"O.K." Frenchy answers back.

"Cum for me" Diamond adds one more time.

"Ooh, I'm gonna cum" Frenchy shouts out.

"Cum on" Diamond tells her as she focuses on her clit.

Frenchy moans louder and louder as she tenses up and humps Diamonds face.

"I'm Cumming" she screams out loud.

"Cum on" Diamond answers back.

"Ooh, shit" Frenchy screams aloud as she starts to tremble.

Diamond starts to slow down and lick around her clit because she knows that it is super sensitive after she Cums. She starts to kiss her thighs and around her stomach. Then she kisses all the way up to her breast and up to her lips.

Frenchy kisses Diamond passionately and never thinks twice about she may be falling for her. Diamond caresses her as she can feel the heart felt feelings coming from Frenchy.

Frenchy starts to cry.

"Whats wrong" Diamond asks her.

"Nothing, I am just so happy right now" she answers.

"I think I love you" Frenchy tells Diamond.

Diamond looks at her in silence and hesitates. Then she leans to her, kisses her and tells her "I love you too Frenchy".

They hug each other and squeeze each other so tight that they both start to laugh out loud.

"Lets get dressed and go out for a walk" Diamond tells Frenchy.

"Sure" Frenchy answers.

They get up and go into the bathroom and turn on the water in the shower. They both get into the shower and wash each other. Then they both dry each other off and start to put their clothes on.

"You sure look cute in those jeans" Frenchy tells Diamond.

"Thank you" Diamond answers as they finish getting dressed.

"You know I remember hooking you up with some cute gear" Diamond tells Frenchy as she smiles at her.

"I remember" Frenchy tells her.

Just then there's a knock at the door. "Knock, knock, knock" Goodnight knocks on the door.

Frenchy goes over to the door and looks in the peep hole. It's Goodnight, she thinks to herself and then she opens the door.

"Hey Good, Come on in" she tells him.

"How are you" he answers back as he walks in thru the door.

"I'm good thanks" she tells him as she closes the door. Good sees that she is not alone and Diamond is there.

"Well hello there" Good greets Diamond.

"Hello" Diamond answers back.

"Don't you look lovely" he tells her.

"Why thank you and you don't look so bad yourself" she tells him.

Frenchy gets a lil jealous and tells Good to watch it but Good pays her no mind. He walks over to Diamond and takes her by the hand.

"And what is your name" he asks Diamond while holding her hand.

"Diamond" she answers him as she is caught off guard.

"Diamond this is Good" Frenchy tells her before Good could say anything else. Good raises her hand to his lips and kisses her hand.

"Very nice to meet you" he says after kissing her hand.

Frenchy walks over to Good and gives him a great big hug as if she was trying to take his attention away from Diamond. Then she gives him a great big wet smack in the lips and says "thanks for coming over babe".

"Oh you're welcome" he answers while still holding Diamonds hand. At that moment Frenchy realizes that she had sandwiched Good right in the middle of her and Diamond. Then she also noticed that Good had Diamonds hand against his pants feeling him up.

She wants to say something but something is not letting her speak. She is kind of excited with both of her loves together with her and Diamond is not saying anything neither.

Diamond looks Frenchy is her eyes letting her know that it's ok as she grabs Goodnights penis and Frenchy kisses Good and then she leans over and kisses Diamond.

Good gets excited and his penis starts to get harder and harder and then Diamond leans over and kisses Good too.

Good starts to peck both of them one by one and then the girls peck each other. They all work themselves over to the bed and then Good pushes Diamond down on the bed and grabs Frenchy and gives her a long wet kiss.

Frenchy starts to take his belt loose and then Diamond joins in and unbuttons his pants too as he pulls off his shirt. Then Frenchy pushes him down on the bed and they both attack him and pull his under shorts off.

They both want the real thing and they want him to give it to them right now.

They both climb over him and one kisses his lips and the other starts on his chest. Diamond goes down and grabs his penis and starts to stroke it.

Good starts to moan as it feels so good to him and they both love every moment of his naked erect penis.

"I want you in my mouth" Frenchy tells him.

"Yes" he answers back "Please".

So she licks on his penis slowly as if she wants to tease him and then she puts the head into her warm mouth. He tells her that it feels so good and she starts to suck on it gently.

Diamond pulls off her shirt and puts her breast in his face. Good loves her beautiful breast and starts to lick on them as he grabs them. He squeezes her tits and starts to suck on them one at a time.

He is really loving this and Frenchy knows it because his penis is getting so hard and stiff as she keeps on sucking just a little bit more aggressively.

Diamond goes down and meets Frenchy at Goods penis and tells her "Let me have some" as she grabs his hard woody.

Frenchy gladly gives it to her as Diamond is a real pro at sucking dick. She starts licking, stroking, sucking and twisting it all at the same time. She is really working it and Frenchy is watching and taking mental notes.

Frenchy then stands up and takes her clothes off while not taking her eyes off of Diamond putin in some work on Good.

She climbs on the bed after listening to Good moan and groan and then she lifts her leg over him as if she wants to ride him like a horse.

She tells him "I want you inside me" as she scoots down closer to his penis and Diamond pulls it out of her mouth and guides Frenchy's ass toward it with one hand and points Goodnights penis toward her pussy with the other.

She slowly puts the head in and then Frenchy eases the rest inside of her wet horny vagina. Diamond kisses Frenchy on her back as she starts to stroke Good.

Diamond then changes positions and moves up to Goods face and starts to kiss him.

Then she kisses Frenchy in the mouth and then back to Goods lips.

Then she tells Frenchy to let her have some and Frenchy jumps off the dick and she jumps on it and rides it like long ranger.

Frenchy moves her position up to Goods face and starts to kiss him in the mouth as she masturbates at the same time.

All three of them are moaning and groaning and getting louder and louder.

Diamond says "I think I'm gonna cum" and Good tells her "Me too".

"Me three" says Frenchy and then not a few seconds later they all cum one right after another in a chain reaction.

"Oh" "Ooh" "Yes" "Mmm Hmm" Yhea baby" "That's it" "Yep" "Ooh yhea" "Mmmm" "Shit" "Mutha Fucka" "Fuck me"......

The end

Other Books by David Broussard

Mr. Goodnight

Amazon.com and

www.createspace.com/3592754

Ebooks

www.smashwords.com/books/view/55395